Snail-Shell

J. H. Langille

Bigwater Classics™

Bigwater Publishing
Caledonia, Michigan

Snail-Shell Harbor was originally published in 1870 by
Henry Hoyt, Boston

This reprint is a *Bigwater Classics*™ Edition
Copyright © 2001 by Donna Winters including front and back matter
and editorial changes to the original text.

Bigwater Classics™ is a trademark of Bigwater Publishing,
 P.O. Box 177, Caledonia, MI 49316

Library of Congress Control Number 00-136122
ISBN 0-923048-52-9

Printed in the United States of America

01   02   03   04   05   06   07 / /   9   8   7   6   5   4   3   2   1

A Note to Readers from Editor Donna Winters

In preparing this edition of *Snail-Shell Harbor*, I have endeavored to remain as true to the original novel in both text and illustrations as possible.

The front cover bears the look of the original novel, including color, texture, decorations, and type.

Decorative chapter heads have been preserved as much as possible. A few required alteration for clarity in printing.

The text is a faithful reprint of the original in its entirety, including nineteenth-century spelling, grammar, punctuation, capitalization, and hyphenation that may appear incorrect to today's readers.

At the end of the story are advertisements for books available from the original publisher in 1870. This section is included only as an item of curiosity. The books are not available for purchase. Immediately following this section is a listing of titles currently offered by Bigwater Publishing.

Thank you for your interest in this reprinted edition about Michigan's past!

FRONTISPIECE.—See page 25.

Snail-Shell Harbor.

BY

J. H. LANGILLE.

BOSTON:
PUBLISHED BY HENRY HOYT,
No. 9 CORNHILL.

TO

SETH SLOAN, M.D.,

AN ESTEEMED FRIEND AND RELATIVE,

𝕿𝖍𝖎𝖘 𝖁𝖔𝖑𝖚𝖒𝖊

IS AFFECTIONATELY DEDICATED

BY

THE AUTHOR.

PREFACE.

THIS volume is a picture from life, as recently seen by the author in the region referred to. May it awaken an interest in behalf of that important part of our country, and especially in its moral and religious wants!

J. H. L.

CONTENTS.

CONTENTS.

CONTENTS.

CONTENTS.

SNAIL-SHELL HARBOR.

CHAPTER I.

The Harbor, and the People who lived there.

N the north-western coast of Lake Michigan, a narrow point of land bends around towards the west and north, somewhat like the curling tube of a snail-shell. From this peculiar shape, the smooth sheet of clear water which fills the cove was, by the early settlers of those parts, called Snail-Shell Harbor.

There is scarcely a more romantic spot in all this

15

region. The point itself, with its short, dense growth of cedars and white birch, pushing to the very edge of an abrupt shore of bright limestone, forms a motley contrast with the tall, dark green forest clothing the higher land, which rolls up against the horizon beyond. The water is clear as crystal. Fish more than twenty feet from the surface seem near enough to be reached with the hand, and pebbles gleam as if within a show-case. The eastern curve of the harbor, formed by the mainland, is a continuous bluff of limestone, rising up out of the water like a perpendicular wall some hundred and fifty feet. Its strata are smoothly cut and clearly marked, and look like a huge piece of masonry. Shrubbery has grown out of its chinks; and vines creep about it in various directions, and hang in rich festoons. At its base, fragments of stone, shaped like broken columns, rise to a considerable height out of the water.

About two miles farther south is Indian Bluff. It

reaches out a long distance into the lake, continues its height of four hundred feet to the extreme point, and is covered with a short, dense growth of dark evergreen down to the water's edge.

Between this and Snail-Shell Harbor is a large inlet, around the head of which curves a beautiful beach of yellow sand, densely packed, and broad enough for several horsemen to ride abreast. The sand bottom extends like an immense inclined plane, a long distance into the lake, making an admirable bathing place.

Add now to the scene a few islands off the mainland, and our idea of the locality is made out.

The scattered population of this region is a strange mixture, from different communities and nationalities. They represent many States of the Union, as well as England, Ireland, France, and various parts of Germany. For the most part, they are by no means an elevated class of people; but seem, rather, like stray fragments of humanity, which, by some strange combination of circumstances, have drifted to these far off shores of our country.

The season is too cold and short, and the soil too unproductive, to make farming profitable; so the people are occupied, for the most part, with fishing. In more thriving communities, some miles distant, lumbering is quite a business; while farther northwest is the celebrated region of iron-mines.

At the time when our narrative begins, Snail-Shell Harbor contained but one family; and there were no neighbors nearer than two miles in any direction; while all the families, for ten miles distant, would scarcely have filled a country school-house.

The home of this solitary family was a long, narrow, low, log-hut, in the inner most curve of the harbor, and close to the water's edge. One end was the dwelling, and the other was a store; for this was the commercial point for more than twenty miles around. An additional small shed near by, for the cow, made up the buildings of the locality.

The head of the family, and the merchant, was an odd and mysterious character. More than fifty years of age, he had been known for the last seven years in these parts as a Norwegian by birth: back of that his history was wrapt in a mystery; and he was perfectly mute, as to adding any information to the various conjectures of his neighbors. "Sandy" was the only name he had reported for himself; and by this he was known more familiarly than any other man, for many miles distant.

Of about middling height, he was thick, heavy-limbed, and square-built; his naturally awkward movements being increased by the use of a wooden stub, instead of a right leg, which he had left behind him somewhere in his mysterious journey through life, no one knew where. Some of the shrewder men suggested, in a quiet way, that it might have been lost in some piratical encounter, with which they supposed his former life to have been connected. His large head, bushy hair, full, swarthy face; coarse features, made ruder by continual contact with the worse sides of life; and his large gray eyes, which never changed in their cold, dark expression,—all gave him an air quite in keeping with the unhappy suspicions concerning the obscurity of his earlier years. Nor did his present life improve men's opinions. To the small but honorable trade in groceries, dry-goods, and hardware, demanded by this sparse community, he added the horrible traffic of intoxicating drinks; for which many spent more of the scanty supply of money within their reach than for the real wants of life. Sandy had no troubles of conscience. Sharp in a small sphere of trade, humorous and even vulgar in conversation, obliging by nature and more so from policy, he could barter in corn-meal and whiskey, gamble and swear, all to the same purpose. To him, sensual gratification and worldly gain were the highest good. Beyond these, he never seemed to think.

But the moral sentiment of his community was so low, that men were not startled by his immoralities; while certain marks of superior power, which he showed, elevated him into respectability. Wholly uneducated, he could conduct his entire business without the aid of either arithmetic or ledger. His command of a boat was perfectly wonderful. He seemed to be on perfectly good terms with all the winds and the waves. No one ever knew him to be afraid of a storm, or to have a mishap in any emergency.

Some five years since, he had married an Irish widow, with a young family of three sons. Short, slender, straight, of fair complexion, deep hazel eyes, and heavy, dark hair, she wore a constant look of carefulness and anxiety, not without certain marks of lingering disappointments. Her active, tidy habits, good English, and general taste, showed that she had, at some time, come in contact with the higher walks of life. She had seen happier days in times gone by, and was in many respects by far Sandy's superior. There was much wonderment at her marrying the rude stranger; but the miserable life and death of a drunken husband, with three small children on her hands, and nothing to support them, had reduced her ambition to the bare necessities of life.

Tom, Frank, and Harry was the order in which the boys were known; and their ages were, respectively, fourteen, twelve, and nine. Harry, the youngest, was a babe of seven months when his father died of delirium-tremens. He was a bright child, overflowing with life and activity, and a genuine good nature,—the star of the household.

What was there here to give healthful employment to these young hands, and train such restless, growing minds into a fit sense of life? Almost nothing,—even worse than nothing. Absolutely

22

idle more than half the time, and surrounded by the lowest influences, how much of a true humanity could one expect from them?

CHAPTER II.

Strangers are Landed.

THE harbor, with the settlements adjoining, was in every respect a community by itself. However thrilling and profound the interests that might stir the great world in general, they seldom ever reached this remote corner of mankind. No thoroughfare disturbed the quiet. No newspaper brought sensations. The harbor was the centre of trade and public affairs. Here every face was known, and almost every character. The appearance of a stranger was a most uncommon occurrence, and excited the deepest curiosity.

It was early in spring. The great sheets of ice, over which men, horses, and oxen had come and gone throughout the long winter, had groaned and heaved, and broken into all shapes and sizes, and drifted out slowly into the great waste of waters beyond. The huge drifts of snow upon the hills had reluctantly melted away under the growing warmth of the long cloudless days, and rushed down the sharp-cut ravines, chiming in with the song of birds, and all the voices of spring, which echo like the steps of summer in the distance. The familiar boats of the different bays and nooks in the vicinity had just begun to appear in the harbor, when a strange-looking sloop was tied to the wharf, and landed a company of strange gentlemen, dressed in the latest cut of fashion, and moving with all the airs of thorough and extensive habits of business.

The whole family in the log-hut are on the alert. Sandy is all animation, and thumps about with his wooden leg even more briskly than usual. Mrs. Sandy peers through the small window of her humble apartment; and the boys go down to the wharf, and examine the boat, and, coming back, scan the strangers from head to foot. And they, in turn, examine the coast, sound the harbor, and make excursions among the thick woodlands, which undulate in every direction from the shore; and form their decision.

Snail-Shell Harbor is no longer to be the quiet spot we have just been describing. A new enterprise is afoot, which is to bring to pass a thorough revolution. One of the large iron-mines near Lake Superior is about to smelt its ore in its own region; and, as they find it easier to take the ore to the wood than the wood to the ore, they will purchase the immense tract of woodland in the vicinity, and make the harbor the point of business. Henceforth, it is to be one of the most active communities in all the region round about.

"A grand thing for you, sir. The business will start right up, and make a little fortune for you," congratulated one of the gentlemen, as he put a roll of greenbacks in Sandy's hand, as a recognition of his special claim to this spot, by way of pre-emption.

"Can't tell vat you big fish vill do wid us little ones," replied Sandy, half in jest, and half in earnest.

It was quite evident that he was not especially pleased with the prospect of becoming second to other men in the domain of which he had so long been king.

"You'll soon get out of the log-house, when the money begins to pour in here," continued the first speaker in a tone of flattery.

"Veree goode: ve'll see," added Sandy, with an air of shrewd misgiving, notwithstanding the flattering prospects just alluded to.

"You shall have your share of business of some

kind," promised another gentleman of the company, with an emphasis and air of candor which were not unsatisfactory to Sandy, as he cast off the moorings of the sloop from the wharf, by way of compliment to the gentlemen going on board.

"Goode words. Time 'ill show," he muttered half aloud to himself, or to the boys, who, with him, were watching the elegant little craft as her white sails, finely filled, disappeared around the point.

CHAPTER III.

"The Northern Light."

NLY six weeks had passed; but great changes had been wrought in and about the harbor. The short, thick growth of cedars and white birch showed general signs of havoc. A long dock had been constructed; several schooners had landed large quantities of building-materials; and houses and barns of the ruder class had been built. An immense smelting-stack was going up; and coal-pits were beginning to smoke on the sides of the high hill which overlooked the harbor. The

29

whole region echoed with the sound of axes and hammers. More men were constantly coming; and new points of work were starting every day.

It was a clear June morning. The air was cool, and so refreshing and invigorating, that one involuntarily took long, deep breaths. The sky was deep and cloudless; and the whole lake sparkled like a sea of stars. Every thing was particularly lively this morning; for to-day was to be a new era in the community. "The Northern Light," one of the finest steamboats on the lake, was expected every hour, to bring large re-enforcements to the business.

In due time, the cloud of smoke, and the large hull, appeared in the distance, among the host of fishing-boats which displayed their white sails against the horizon. Great was the excitement when the steam-whistle blew at the mouth of the harbor, and the large boat, bristling with passengers, moved up with all her dignity, and cast her moorings upon the dock. Greater still was the surprise when the cargo was opened up. First in order came a hundred horses, large, sleek, and of all colors.

"Big as elephants! Fat as seals! Do for a show! Finer sight I never seed!" exclaimed Sandy with emotion.

"See there!" cried one of the boys in utmost curiosity, as trucks, wagons, and working-implements in many colors, and fresh from the manufactories, were paraded upon the dock.

"What's that?" cried another, as an immense steam-engine for the smelting-stack was pushed out from the steamer's broadside with much difficulty, and with loud shouts from the sailors.

"That's an *iron* horse!" said the captain, who stood near, and stopped just long enough to utter the words, between his stentorian orders to the hands, who were covering the dock with building-materials of various kinds.

An "iron horse" was something new to the boys; and they were truly puzzled in trying to find some point of resemblance between the huge piece of machinery and a real horse.

Meanwhile the strangers had landed, and were inquiring as to the various items of interest about the place.

"Great deal to see here," spoke Sandy, who could appreciate all the points of interest in the vicinity; and at once offered his service as conductor-in-chief of the company.

He hobbled around in perfect excitement. His tongue, always glib and oily, was amazingly eloquent; and he showed a degree of politeness of which no one had ever before suspected him capable. He called the attention of the company to the various nooks and haunts; and they collected a whole cabinet of little curiosities, and carried off evergreens in abundance. They thought Sandy himself, with his broad Norwegian brogue and odd humor, as much an object of curious interest as any thing the locality afforded.

The cargo was landed; the passengers were "all aboard;" and the steamer was moving majestically out of the harbor, with the understanding, that, henceforth, she was to touch regularly once a week at this point, on her round trip to the principal business-localities of the lake regions.

CHAPTER IV.

A Sacred Messenger.

N addition to the regular landing of the steamer, schooners came occasionally; steam-tugs belonging to the company plied constantly between the harbor and adjoining points connected with its new business.

The great healthfulness of the northern lake-regions, the beautiful and romantic scenery which abounds on every hand, and the many resources of amusement in hunting, fishing, &c., bring many visitors from different parts of our country to spend their summer months here. Green Bay, Escanaba, Negannee, and Marquette are among the principal resorts, and are places of much interest. Now that the harbor was becoming known as a locality which abounds in fine scenery, and a new and important point of business, many found their way thither from the surrounding public resorts, on tugs and scows, to spend a few hours in rowing, fishing, or observing the rapidly-increasing business of the iron company.

One morning late in June, when a few fleecy clouds, transfigured by a clear sun, gleamed like streaks of pearl on the pure azure beyond; when great varieties of wild flowers, curious in forms and colors, began to peer in beds of moss, to creep over rocks, and hang from cliffs; and the harbor, smooth as a mirror, reflected tree and rock and bluff and hill until every surrounding object became double,—there appeared in the harbor a solitary stranger, of quite unusual and marked appearance. Evidently he was not altogether a man of business nor of pleasure. Plain and neat in dress, young, pale, and delicate, contemplative rather than demonstrative, he made a quiet visit, took a full observation of the moral as well as the business aspects of the place, and in a humble way delivered a sacred message, the effect of which was to be felt in after-years. For some time, he had been fishing near the dock, from the side of the tug which had brought him. He had seen the rush and commotion of business, and heard the vulgarity and profanity of the common conversation. From that logical association of ideas by which we receive a general impression from but a partial view of principal facts, he felt that this place was given over to worldly gain while God was wholly forgotten; and, like Him who wept over the doomed city, his heart was moved with compassion for the souls about him.

Like his Master, "who went about doing good,"

preaching the Gospel even to the wicked Samaritan woman at the well, he, with remarkable skill, spoke of Jesus, and the way of life, to everyone he met. The steward on the tug, the captain, and all the hands, had been set to thinking by his quiet and timely suggestions. Bad language had been quietly rebuked, and the life hereafter had been solemnly referred to. Sandy, while thumping around on the dock, indulging his usual freedom in profanity, and endeavoring to draw attention to his saloon near by, had felt pricks of conscience, and a sense of shame all together new to him, while listening to the strange accents of a purer spirit, perhaps, than he had ever met before. Leading employees of the company, and workmen of the lower class, had met the same influence. Many new reflections were started; and more than one felt a strange spiritual hunger.

There was a pattering of bare feet upon the dock. Harry, the youngest and most promising

37

member of Sandy's family, left free to go and come when and where he pleased, was absent from the harbor when the tug came in; and had just appeared to take his usual observation of the arrival. His face was fresh as a rose washed out with dew. Whatever were his marks of poor breeding, he was evidently gifted of nature with a bright mind and a healthy body. The stranger, who had just drawn in a bass over the stern of the tug, was the principal object of notice; and, with that instinct by which children so readily detect a congenial nature, Harry was unconsciously drawn towards him. First, he sat down on a pile of lumber on the edge of the dock: then he leaned over against the side of the tug; and finally climbed on board, and sat down close to the stranger's elbow.

There had not been silence all this time. A kindly and interesting conversation had magnetized and attracted Harry more than anything else. He was not naturally bold or obtrusive; but somehow he felt perfectly free, and strangely happy, in the presence of the new visitor.

An expression, half of surprise, half of confidence, beamed in his large, deep, blue eyes, as the stranger grasped his fat hand playfully.

"Do you like me?" inquired the little fellow somewhat seriously, after looking fairly into his friend's face and eyes for several minutes.

"I like all little boys that are good," was the reply, with a smile. "I guess you're good, are you not?"

That was a strange question to Harry, and he could only laugh awkwardly in reply.

"Good boys don't use any bad words," continued the stranger. "Don't play or work on Sunday."

"Pa swears," replied the little fellow. "And Tom and Frank."

"Oh, how sorry I am for them!" added the gentleman, with an expression of sorrow, that brought a grave, thoughtful look to every feature of the child's face. "It is very wicked to sear."

This was startling news to our little friend. Oaths of every kind had been common to almost all conversation he had ever heard; and he had never been taught that they were wicked. Nor had he ever learned anything about the Lord's day. He had never heard "the sound of the church-going bell;" and the voice of prayer and praise, common to church and Sunday school, and so many families circle throughout our land, he had never known. To his life, all days of the week were alike, except that, on Sunday, the household drove a larger trade in every article of exchange, liquors not accepted: for there was not a church, or Sunday school, or family altar, for many miles around; and Sunday was the day to leave fishing and the farm, and go to the harbor to trade, gossip, and drink. Nor had the new business wrought any marked change. The men it brought there seemed all ungodly. If the Sabbath had any thing less of labor than other days of the week, it had more of boat-riding, hunting, and loafing.

"Do you know who made you?" inquired the stranger, holding up the child's hand and plump arm, half covered with a torn shirt sleeve, as the object of contemplation.

"Didn't I grow, like the trees and the flowers?"

"Yes, my dear, very much like the trees and flowers; but who made *them* grow?"

The child looked puzzled. A new query was breaking upon him, which his untutored mind was not able to answer.

"God made you," added the stranger, with a solemn, earnest look.

"Who is God?" questioned Harry, his whole face radiant with inquiry. Times without number, he had heard the name of God taken in vain, and even himself had learned to repeat it in moments of passion; but never before had he known it as the name of Him who made us.

"God is he who made the world, and all that is in it," answered the stranger; "and the sun and the moon and the stars."

"Where is he?" continued the child.

"He is in heaven; and though we cannot see that place, or know where it is, we know that, somehow, God is everywhere."

"Can he see *us?*"

"He sees every thing. He hears what we say. He knows even our thoughts. He sees us in the darkness, as well as in the light."

Harry sat motionless and speechless, and looked steadfastly into the face of the wonderful messenger, his eyes dilating with earnestness and suffused with tears. Never was the word of truth preached to a truer listener. There was no cherishing of deep-seated, sinful habits, no sophistry of argument, or clouds of doubt; nothing but that humble confidence and profound sincerity with which "a little child" receives the kingdom of God.

The speaker felt that the Holy Spirit helped both his hearer and himself, as he briefly related the account of the creation, showed forth our sin and ruin, portrayed the life and death of Christ, and explained the way of faith in him, as the only salvation from "the worm which never dieth, and the fire that is not quenched."

The captain stepped on board, the whistle blew, and the tug moved out of the harbor, bearing away the mysterious stranger.

Harry stood on the dock, and watched the tug till it turned the point and disappeared; and then went his way, to ponder upon the strange things he had heard.

A deep impression had been made. The seed had been sewn in an honest heart. But could anything be hoped for, in the case of one apparently so wholly separated from the influences necessary to the nurture of Christian truth? one who could not read a word, did not even know one letter from

another, had never seen a Bible or any other religious work, and, until the present, had never met
one who feared God? We shall see what God can
do for those whose hearts are open to receive him.

CHAPTER V.

A New Place and a New Name.

I N the region of our story, summer and autumn are not, as in many other parts of our country the crown of the year. The verdure of the fields is not rich, and forest-leaves do not hang in rank clusters of gorgeous greens. But flowers, the most benevolent part of all the vegetable kingdom, and which love to smile even in desert places, bloom wild here in abundance; and, to one from ordinary climates, they are very rare and delicate.

Following so short and cool a summer, autumn is not very fruitful; and the early frosts blast the hills ere the leaves can ripen into the bright autumn tints of the climes where the eye can range through all shades of green, yellow, scarlet, and purple.

In these parts, winter is worth all the rest of the year. The lakes become like seas of glass. Heavy falls of dry, pure snow shroud the trees, overhang the rocks in curious, curling shapes, as if some skilful artist's hand had fashioned them into endless forms of taste and beauty, and anon rise from hillsides like towns and palaces of purest marble. Then by some sudden freak, the Winter-King mysteriously combines snow and rain, clothing every rock, tree, and shrub, till, on some sunny morning, one awakes to find nature perfectly transfigured. All this gives an endless charm to the long months of storm, not to speak of sleigh-riding on streets of pure enamel, and flying, on the wings of the wind, across broad acres of transparent glass.

But whatever the comparative interest of the seasons, they had each, in turn, wrought a great change at the harbor. Only one year had passed since the new business had been located here; and yet a stranger might scarcely recognize the place. The smelting-stack, a huge pile of dark-colored buildings, had been completed; and the flame of the furnace was rolling up many feet above its highest point. It stood fair in the middle of the harbor and of the dock. At the right was a long line of coal-pits, built of brick, in very much the shape of large haystacks, and plastered over with white mortar. These were constantly at work, making immense quantities of wood into charcoal, to feed the great shaft of flame in the furnace. And they were aided by immense pits, which were kept constantly burning, several miles back in the woods. Just beyond the pits, at the right of the furnace, was a large lime-kiln; which made great quantities of rock into lime, to supply what is called a flux in melting the iron-ore. The lime, put into the furnace with the ore, makes the melted iron come out purer. Near the kiln, a company of men were constantly blasting the rock for its supply; and a general alarm it was to the whole community, when the report of the explosion echoed among the hills and along the shore, like the firing of an immense cannon, and great volleys of rock splashed out into the harbor in every direction.

At the left of the furnace, and near the dock, a large and elegant store had been built, which, but for Sandy's many friends and courteous business habits, would have been a sad blow to his establishment; especially as the sale of liquors, which had always been one of the largest branches of his trade, was now forbidden by the company. But what he lacked in this respect was made up to him by odd jobs of boating, which the new enterprise of the place afforded.

Near the extremity of the point, a large and

tasteful dwelling had been erected for the general overseer employed by the company. Along the elevation back of the store was a line of smallish brown framed-houses, for the better class of employees. On the west side of the point, towards the sand-beach, was a long row of log-houses, occupied by the poorer classes of workmen.

Thus in one year, had a village of several hundred inhabitants sprung up; and, every week, "The Northern Light" found several hundred tons of pig-iron ready for the market.

This new place numbered a small circle of quite respectable and ambitious citizens. In addition to the general overseer, there was a physician, and a number of clerks in the store, as also a number of captains of tugs, and superintendents of the various departments of the general business.

They hardly liked the old and vulgar name of Snail-Shell Harbor, so they called the new community "Ironville." But either from its natural fitness, or from the force of habit, the old name refused to give way to the new one. While the designation of the post-office, and the address of all items of mail was "Ironville," almost every one persisted in calling the place, "Snail-Shell Harbor."

CHAPTER VI.

A Sunday at the Harbor.

WE have observed with interest the outward aspects of our little village, and its rapid growth in business. But there is an inward character to every community, which holds something of the same relation to the external as that of the soul to the body. This inner life no day of the week so fully reveals as Sunday. Then men feel comparatively free from those stern necessities of life, which, on other days of the week, compel them to a wholesome industry. Thus the day so much needed for rest and devotion is turned by the wicked into an occasion of idleness and temptation.

For a better acquaintance with the harbor, let us spend a Sunday there; and, to get the best point of view, we will enter the residence of Dr. Sprague, who occupies one of the smallish brown houses before referred to. We shall easily distinguish it from the rest in that long row; for it has a white porch in front by which any child in the village can point it out.

Only two—the doctor and his wife—make up the regular family. But at present, Miss Elliott, his wife's sister, is a transient member of the household. She has just arrived to spend a few weeks, partly for a visit, and partly for her health.

The doctor is an eccentric man. Tall, slender, straight, blue eyed, well sunburnt, his brown hair, and thin dark whiskers slightly sprinkled with gray, he is free and easy in his manner, and quite talkative. You will feel at home; for he will not awe you with his dignity, and he is remarkably kind and social.

He will not be afraid to speak lest your words should be criticised; for he talks as carelessly and jocosely as a school-boy, and makes you feel that you ought to do the same. In no part of his house will you be conscious of any restraint. You will be as free in the dining room, or in the kitchen, as in the parlor. In short, you will be perfectly free to do as you please; and the doctor will do every thing in his power to accommodate you.

His wife is a short, plump, tidy woman, with a kindly face and a few words; keeping every thing in its place, and making the entire household machinery move on without the least jar or friction.

Miss Elliott is a small, fair, light haired, dark eyed, delicate young lady of about twenty-three. Her well trained intellect, and sensitive, poetic nature, make her keenly alive to all the romance and beauty of the harbor; but her taste and piety are constant martyrs to the rudeness and vice by which she is surrounded.

"How quiet every thing is this morning!" she remarked, as she sat by the open window, and looked up and down the street, and towards the store and the dock, without seeing a single person astir.

It was a calm, clear morning. Scarcely the rustle of a leaf, or the note of a bird, broke the stillness.

"The Paddies spreed so hard and so late last night, that they haven't got around yet this morning," added the doctor. "Did you hear the music over on Shanty Street? They kept me awake till after midnight." Like all communities of a low moral town, the people here are excessively given to amusement. Among them are a few third or fourth rate players of the violin; and they generally manage to start a dance and carousal every Saturday night, which lasts well on towards the morning. Then the Sabbath is a day of drowsiness and satiety.

"Neither school, nor schoolhouse, nor church, nor public worship!" continued Miss Elliot in a tone of sympathy and regret. "In the absence of all these nobler influences, so absolutely necessary to enlighten and stimulate the conscience of even the best communities, what is to become of this collection of human beings, so low in the moral scale? Men have no fear of God before their eyes, and children are growing up in ignorance and vice."

"A bad state of things, truly," admitted the doctor; "but I can scarcely see any prospect for anything better. All real estate is in the hands of the company. Residents regard themselves as but transient, and are slow to invest in any public matter. If anything is done towards accommodations for intellectual or moral improvement, it must be by the company. But in such matters they have no interests. They are wealthy merchants in Eastern cities, and see nothing in human beings but a machinery to make money. To this end every thing is arranged. The bone and muscle of every man is taxed to the utmost. Through high rents for houses, enormous profits on goods out of the store, and various other channels, as much as possible of the wages paid out is brought back again into the original fund."

As the sun rose higher, children began to appear about the premises. By and by men sauntered out, gathered in little knots to smoke their tobacco, tell vulgar stories, and discuss the various items of town-gossip. A closer observation showed that some were at work. As the day wore away, others returned from fishing and hunting excursions. And the great shaft of the furnace rolled up its flame all day long, just as on other days of the week.

The day was drawing to a close, and the doctor's family had just sat down to tea, when there was an uncommonly loud rap at the door.

"Tell the doctor to come quick! A man over here is most killed," cried a large Irishman, who stood at the door puffing and panting, as the servant hurriedly opened it.

As quickly as possible, the doctor was under-way, followed by nearly all the men and boys in the village, who rushed with all speed to see what had happened.

Near the sand-beach, and just outside the juris-diction of the company, was a liquor shop, which had sprung up to occupy the field vacated by Sandy. This new man in the business was greatly annoyed by trading-boats, which began to be attracted by the growth of the community, and which invariably carried a sufficient supply of liquors along with their dry-goods and groceries. He was determined to contest his ground. So there was a constant warfare between him and every boat-merchant who landed within his reach. To-day he had met one of these fellow-competitors

57

with special abuse. He had gone down to the shores and warned him off, in language by no means polite. A sharp altercation followed, thoroughly seasoned with blackguardism and oaths, and ended by the boatman thrusting a pike into the side of his antagonist, wounding him badly and breaking several of his ribs.

The commotion had somewhat subsided and the doctor, having done what he could for his patient, had returned home.

"A pretty hard community this!" he exclaimed with a decided emphasis, after relating to the household the particulars of the late occurrence. "Very few decent men come here."

"I thought the company had forbidden the sale of liquors here?" suggested Miss Elliot.

"So they have," added the doctor. "Not for any moral purpose, however,—purely for economy. But it is a practical failure. The great body of the men still drink. They manage to get it somehow.

Boats land slily in the night, and supply a regular class of customers; and old topers smuggle it from adjoining markets. There's plenty of it here, that's certain; and men carry the most barbarous marks in consequence. Some one has a piece of an ear bit off, or the first joint of a finger. Another has a rib or two broken, or even an eye knocked out. I'm not religious myself; but if any preacher could be found, who could scare these rascals half out of their wits, and make them lead a better life, I would hold up both hands for him."

Miss Elliot smiled at the doctor's crude idea of the nature of morality, and of the result to be expected from religious teaching.

"Very few become good by scaring," she added modestly. "The grace of God is what they need. The question is, Are we doing what we can to invite them to it?"

"I attend to their bodies. That is enough for one man; about all I can do."

59

The doctor spoke good-humoredly, but twitched around in his chair, as if a thorn had pricked him somewhere.

"To attend to the bodies of men is, indeed, a great work, and a great responsibility," added Miss Elliot seriously; "but the body is only a lesser part of human beings. Why repair the house, while you care not for the immortal man who lives within it? No one can help the soul so readily as he who helps the body. No one ever cared so tenderly for man's physical wants as Christ. But he did not stop there. Through the body he reached the soul."

This was eloquent preaching. The doctor felt the force of it, and skillfully turned the conversation.

The long, cloudless day had been followed by a gorgeous sunset, shading the clear sky with every tint of crimson, violet, and purple. Twilight had deepened into darkness, and the sounds of day-life had died out of the village streets.

Thus passed a Sabbath at the harbor. Surely, it is no pleasing picture: and yet is it true to life,—nor merely to that of this community, but of many others in the less favored parts of our land.

But when one describes the frivolities and crimes of a people, only the outside can be painted. In the more secluded and inward parts of their life are deeds of darkness and of shame which cannot be put on paper, and of which one would blush even to speak. Such, we have every reason to believe, were not uncommon at the harbor.

CHAPTER VII.

A Glimpse at Sandy's Fireside.

THE harbor was crowded to its utmost capacity. The business was rapidly extending, and constantly called for new recruits, in every department of labor. Now an engineer was wanted, now a collier, or a captain for an additional tug, or twenty or thirty new hands. And, as direct business paid the company better than the mere providing of accommodations, the entire community was pressed into the smallest possible space.

Until very recently, there had been no regularly

announced hotel. All the village kept boarding-house, and gave meals at all hours. But Sandy, whose eye was always keen to detect a new point of business in a small way, thought he saw a want of the times, and put out a sign,—"house for strangers, visitors, and new-comers." It would command general attention; for it was perched on the house-top, fairly opposite the dock, and painted on a white background, in large, black letters, traced by the owner's inexperienced hand, and fully betraying his want of skill.

However the various newcomers, landed each week by "The Northern Light," might differ in detail, there was one grand characteristic of them all. They were rough and wicked. A man of refined feeling and tender Christian sympathy would have been a speckled bird amidst the flock.

But to-day a gentleman had landed, whose humane features and kindly expression had attract-ed the attention of every child on the wharf, and many besides. He turned out to be the new engineer, expected for some time, and, of course, put up at Sandy's.

We will look in upon him during the evening, for it will give us a glimpse at Sandy's fire-side, and show us the inner life of that queer log-house; the oldest building in the village. We shall do it at the better advantage, too, since Sandy's mercantile business is "closed out," and he, devoting all his attention as landlord, may spend his evening at home.

The inside of the house is as odd as the outside. The first and main floor, excepting the part formerly occupied as a store, is all in one long, narrow room. This is at once kitchen, dining room, saloon, parlor, and sleeping room. It is low, and poorly lighted. The entrance is at the side. At one end is a bed, at the other an immense open fire-place. Long rows of chests and boxes stand in orderly arrangement along the sides. Several stout blocks, sawed off at sufficient length to make seats, stand about the chimney-corners. There is a large square table with cross-legs, and a few home-made chairs. This about completes the furniture.

But, even in a home so rude as this, there are families, who, independent of the elegancies and wealth of the world, could drink constantly from the deepest fountains of domestic joy. Not so with Sandy's household. He himself, indeed, was never without a certain happiness; but it was only the happiness of the brute, which means to eat and drink and sleep. Mrs. Sandy was a careworn, broken-spirited woman, who bore her trials as a necessity, and filled up the insipid days of life with many and excessive labors. The boys had that pleasure which comes to young and healthy bodies in a free, outdoor life. Of higher interests and tender home affections, they knew nothing.

"S'pose you're used to a great dale more and better than this," apologized Mrs. Sandy, very politely to the new-comer, as she arranged him, with her family, around the table loaded down with good cheer, and made still more cheerful by the large fire which blazed on the hearth, and which may be necessary, in this climate, even in midsummer.

"No fear, madam," kindly rejoined the gentleman. "Every thing is as neat as a new pin, and I am really hungry. This cool has been better to me than a dose of stomach-bitters."

Surely, with a good stomach, there was no need of misgivings; for the table contained a breakfast, dinner, and supper all together. Mrs. Sandy seemed to have put on every thing that could be thought of without the least regard to formality. This was in part from her natural generosity, and in part from the feeling of reverence for the stranger which she could not explain.

About every human being there is a certain moral atmosphere, of which even a stranger, if he be observing, is conscious at the first contact.

"I never has trouble 'bout eatin'," grunted Sandy in his peculiar rough, half-guttural tone of voice.

Certainly not. To this his broad shoulders bore ample testimony, as well as his manner of eating, which made the stranger think of a people mentioned by the great apostle, "whose God was their belly."

"Dubaccy, eh?" suggested Sandy, offering his guest an outfit for smoking, as they seated themselves at the fireside after supper.

"I never use tobacco. Don't believe in it," returned the stranger.

"Fine! fine!" added Sandy, as he rolled out the smoke most lustily.

"Boys, I hope you will never smoke," urged the stranger with great earnestness, as he turned to the lads who sat listening, as if intent on every word.

The boys were far from fulness of conviction on

"Boys, I hope you will never smoke."—Page 67.

the subject; but they never forgot that earnest look.

Supper was over, and every thing cleared up. So Mrs. Sandy took her knitting, and seated herself on one of the blocks near the chimney-corner, thus completing the circle about the fireside.

"Now I must tell you who I am and where I am from," said the stranger; "and then I must talk about something better. My name is Henry Williams. I am from Cleveland, Ohio."

"Vat betther? Ah, ha, ha!" laughed out Sandy humorously, whose curiosity had been piqued by the double promise, and was especially anxious to know the better part.

"The better part is this," continued Mr. Williams: "I have a wife and two little children, whom I want to have under the influence of the precious gospel. But about this better part I am in trouble. You have here no church, no Sunday school, no prayer-meeting, no religious influence whatever."

"Dat's all not vorth a fish-scale!" declared Sandy, striking his fist upon his knee for emphasis.

"Don't you feel the need of Jesus Christ, Sandy?" urged Mr. Williams solemnly.

"Never! Misther Villyoms. I vas saint before you vas borned, an' vill be ven you are hangt. Ha, ha! ha, ha!" shouted the hardened old man, as if feeling that he had put an end to all questioning on that score, as far as he was concerned.

Not that his conscience was free from reproach. This was his method of warding off conviction. He knew that he was a sinner. So do even the heathen.

Mr. Williams went on to speak with sincerity and earnestness.

"The Bible, the book of God, says we are all sinners, and that as such, we can never be at peace. Surely the lives of men prove this. They are like the restless ocean, like the troubled sea that casts up mire and dirt. What horrible crimes do men commit! Can any shameful deed be yet thought of that men have not done? One wonders the sun does not blush to shine on a world so wicked! How few men can be called good in any sense! and if the best of them were placed in the pure light of God's presence, how spotted they would be! Every man's conscience blames him; and, without Christ, who is not afraid to die? You are troubled, Sandy, when you meet death face to face!"

"I tries to run from him," confessed Sandy. "Don't know but the Devil 'ill get me."

A short pause had followed Mr. Williams's direct appeal, and a sharp, awful look, that went through the old man. His conscience answered before he had time to equivocate.

"You see the word of God is right," continued Mr. Williams. "If there were no Christ, our case would be desperate. We should be all shut up to everlasting condemnation. But Christ, the Son of God, has pitied us. He came to the world; became a babe, a child, a man; lived among all kinds of men, healed the sick, comforted the sorrowing, took little children in his arms and blessed them, and raised the dead; labored, hungered, thirsted, and wept; and then gave his body to be beaten and torn, and died hanging on a cross. Men took him down, and put him in a tomb; but he rose again and has ascended to heaven. There he hears our prayers, and is ready to help all who come to him. He calls every one. To the poor he says, Roll your burdens on me. They are heavy, and you are too weak to carry them. I will carry them for you. Trust in me everyday, and ask me for all you need. Don't be afraid. See how I clothe the flowers and feed the birds! You are worth more to me than they. To the wicked he said, Leave off your sins. They are sinking you down and making you wretched. They give you all your trouble. Do they hang to you, so that you cannot shake them off? Do they stick into your very heart, and poison all your thoughts? Come to me. I will save you from your sins. They who come to Christ have nothing to fear. He will make all things work for their good; and, when their bodies fail, he will take them to a world that is better than this,—one where men never sin, never suffer, never die!"

These words broke like a wonderful revelation upon the little audience. It was so much more of the gospel than they have ever heard before. And though they saw but part of its excellence, it sounded like "glad tidings," too good to be believed. But truth always carries conviction and gains confidence.

When the words ended, Sandy was gazing intently into the fire, with a solemn, earnest look that seemed strange on his hard, cold face. He said nothing, and for sometime continued motionless as a statue.

Mrs. Sandy was evidently struggling with emotion, as she pressed her lips together, and wiped away a large tear with the corner of her apron. The

73

message was to her like bread to the hungry, and cold water to a thirsty soul. What a tasteless thing life had been to her! How she had dragged herself through its various rounds, with no object beyond to touch the heart with gladness and hope, and thus quicken the pulses of the soul, but as if driven by some stern and mysterious necessity! Could this message be a morning star on her dark horizon, the harbinger of better days? Certain it was that it had a strange power over her heart, which quickened all her inward longings.

It was that same power that swept like a magnet through a great throng of human hearts, when the Son of man was on the earth; which led poor, suffering, soul-famishing women to press their weary way through the crowd, longing to touch but the fringe of his garment, begging for only the crumbs that fell from the children's table, washing his feet with their tears, and wiping them with the hairs of their head.

The boys sat erect and motionless, and their young faces were full of thought. Harry, the youngest, was more affected than the rest. To him the subject was not so new as to his brothers. He had never forgotten the mysterious stranger, who had made a quiet call at the harbor at the time of the beginning of the new business. That stranger had left the greatest possible impression upon his young mind. The child remembered every feature of his face, the clothes he wore, the tone of his voice, and almost every idea he had uttered. There had not been a day since, in which he had not thought of the great truths he there heard. He had thought of God as everywhere present, to behold the evil and the good, and as knowing the inmost thoughts of his heart. As to the nature of his heart and life, he had had true spiritual conviction, and had felt the heavy weight of guilt. Amid his child-ish sports of the daytime, his reflections would be scattered, and he would laugh and play as merrily

75

as any boy or girl in the village, for never was a child more brimful of life and cheerful good-nature; but when in solitude, or the shadows of night would come on, his thoughtfulness would return, stirring all those musings and tender yearnings, and dark, shadowy fears, which more than one young heart has secretly carried about, while parents and friends saw nothing but thoughtlessness and play. Some nights he had lain awake till a late hour, when the house was so still that he could hear nothing but the beating of his heart. Then he would try to measure eternity, adding life-time to life-time till his comprehension was bewildered, and reflecting upon the wretchedness of that place, "where their worm dieth not, and the fire is not quenched." He would review the deeds of the past day: wonder if he should die before morning; and then, turning around the pillow, wet with his tears and hot from his fevered cheek, would fall asleep wearied out with his reflections.

Mr. Williams was deeply interested; and by that strange power of one heart upon another by which we are made conscious of the feelings of those around us, even when they do not speak, or by that fitness of things which the indwelling spirit of God is ever wont to suggest, he saw that there and then was a field of labor.

"It is getting late; and I am very tired from travelling, and must soon go to bed," said he. "Would you like for me to read and pray with you?" he inquired, drawing a small Bible from his pocket.

"Surely," said Mrs. Sandy with much interest. "It's high time we had the likes o'that in this house."

"Guess it vont hur-r-t anyone," added Sandy as indifferently as possible, moving about with evident uneasiness upon his block, and hitching his wooden leg upon his other knee, as if trying to be perfectly composed.

Mr. Williams read without the least formality.

Instead of reading a chapter through, he made selections of such parts as he thought most appropriate.

First he turned to the 139th Psalm,—"'O Lord, thou hast searched me, and known me. Thou knowest my down-sitting and mine uprising; thou understandest my thought afar off. Thou compassest my path and my lying down, and art acquainted with all my ways. For there is not a word in my tongue, but, low, O Lord, thou knowest it altogether. Thou hast beset me behind and before, and laid thine hand upon me. Such knowledge is too wonderful for me: it is high, I cannot attain unto it. Wither shall I go from thy Spirit? Or wither shall I flee from thy presence? If I ascend up into heaven, thou art there; if I make my bed in hell, behold thou art there. If I take the wings of the morning, and dwell in the uttermost parts of the sea; even there shall thy hand lead me, and thy right hand shall hold me. If I say, surely the darkness shall cover me, even the night shall be light about me. Yea, the darkness hideth not from thee; but the night shineth as the day: the darkness and the light are both alike to thee . . . How precious, also, are thy thoughts unto me, O God! How great is the sum of them! If I should count them, they are more in number than the sand: when I awake, I am still with thee.'"

Then he recited from elsewhere,—"There is none righteous, no, not one. They are all gone out of the way; they are together become unprofitable. There is none that doeth good,—all have sinned and come short of the glory of God." "Except a man be born again, he cannot see the kingdom of God. That which is born of the flesh is flesh; and that which is born of the Spirit is spirit." "He that cometh unto me I will in no wise cast out." "The Spirit and the Bride say, Come. And let him that heareth say, Come. And let him that is a-thirst come; and whosoever will, let him take the water of life freely."

A short, tender, earnest prayer followed. The family seemed a little confused as Mr. Williams began to kneel down. They had never seen anything of the kind before. But Mrs. Sandy's impulse was in the right direction. She followed Mr. Williams, and, for the first time in her life, bowed before God. The children followed her example; and Sandy stood up before the fireplace, leaning forward against the mantle.

The evening was spent, and all retired. Before Mr. Williams could sleep, he had many reflections; but scarcely more than had each member of the family, who had heard such new and strange things, and the gospel so simply, so faithfully preached.

CHAPTER VIII.

A Sad Catastrophe.

R. Sprague was an early riser. It was seldom the sun found him in bed. His business, indeed, was not so pressing as to call him up at so early an hour; but he had a deep-seated conviction that perfect health needed the freshness and vigor of the first of the morning. So he was accustomed to be out before any one else in the village, excepting Sandy. Sometimes he would stroll; sometimes, in summer, he would take a bath in the lake; and sometimes he would ride out on horseback.

He had just risen one morning, and the gray light which streaked the horizon had scarcely brightened into day, when, looking out of the window, he saw Sandy hobbling towards the door with his utmost speed. Knowing that something uncommon was the matter, he hastened and opened the door before he reached it.

"What in the world is the matter, Sandy?" he exclaimed.

"Matter 'nough. Hurry! Come!" cried Sandy, halting suddenly, and beckoning most earnestly for the doctor to follow him.

"Is any one dead?" inquired the doctor, as he sprung to the side of the excited man, and they both hurried away, Sandy leading towards the dock.

"Yes,—woman dead,—drowned, I s'pose."

"Where?"

"Over here. I'll show."

In a few moments, they were in the boat; and Sandy pulled over to the side of the harbor formed

by the main land,—the high wall that rose perpen-
dicularly out of the water.

Here a terrible sight met them. A woman lay in
the shallow water upon the rocks, mangled, bleeding, and torn. She had evidently committed suicide,—had jumped the enormous distance from the
heights above, full a hundred and fifty feet.

The doctor and Sandy had met some one on
their way to the boat; and enough of the conversation had been overheard to awaken a very intense
suspicion. At once the news spread, and in a few
minutes the whole village was roused. Men hurried from every direction. Children ran half-
dressed, and women were out, pale with excitement. By the time the doctor and Sandy returned,
nearly the whole town was on the dock. They
could scarcely get ashore, so eagerly did the whole
crowd press upon them to catch a little further
information as to the catastrophe. It was with the
utmost difficulty that the Dr. and Mr. Alton, who

was the general superintendent of the business of the place, restrained them from cramming the boat, and pushing across to the place of the disaster.

As soon as possible, the legal steps were taken to bring the corpse to the shore.

A number in the crowd at once recognized the face, all bruised and bleeding; but, to the greater part, it was that of an utter stranger.

"Katie!" "Katie O'Donnel!" "Poor Katie!" called out one and another of the women, in surprise and pity.

"Who is she?" inquired the doctor, laying hold of a simple-hearted Irish woman who seemed to know the person, and who, he thought, could tell him a straight story.

"Katie O'Donnel, your honor, sar," she replied, "a stranger,—a poor gairl,—not in town quite two weeks."

"Worked at John Foltenheimer's the first: did stale something, and was turned away," added another tall daughter of Erin unofficially.

"She was at Pat Sharky's, last,—God bless her,—poor soul!" interrupted a third. "Shame on anyone to turn a poor gairl out o' the house! Say what she's coming to now!"

A few expressions like these, passing from lip to lip, quickly enflamed the crowd; and, before any adequate information could be gathered, some had almost come to blows.

John Foltenheimer, who was said to have turned the unfortunate woman out of doors, could scarcely get away with his life; and the doctor hastened the body away to its last place of residence, where it was to be kept till buried.

The case was decided to be one of suicide; and the facts, as nearly as could be ascertained, were as follows: The unhappy woman had come from Chicago a few weeks before, with a very disreputable character, seeking employment as a common house-servant. John Foltenheimer, who boarded a number of the hands in different departments of the business, had employed her; and, after a few days, she was found to have stolen a satchel from some one of the household, and was forthwith dismissed. After that, she had wandered around at several different places, a general victim of crime and suspicion. For some days previous to the present discovery, she had not been seen by any one; and, probably, under the terrible depression of guilt and wretchedness, had taken her own life by throwing herself down from the highest point of the bluff.

One might reasonably expect that so terrible an ending of human life, such fearful results from sin and degradation, would awe the entire community, put a check on vice of every kind, and beget the most solemn moral and religious reflection. But it was surprising to see how slight and temporary was the entire effect. For the most part, only a cold, heartless curiosity was excited, enough to furnish a pretty thorough-going town gossip, and break in upon the general monotony of life. There was a great deal of speculation as to the amount of guilt resting upon John Foltenheimer, and upon various other personages supposed to be more or less connected with the affair; as also concerning the manner in which the funeral should be gotten up; but few reflected upon their own moral condition, or their own mortality. Men even mixed in their oaths as usual, while discussing different points of the new topic.

The funeral was the first in the community, and was highly characteristic of the place. The coffin was a mere rude pine box, nailed together without planing or coloring. The matted locks were scarcely combed out and there was no other shroud than the garments in which the body had first been found. There was no hymn sung, no prayer, no burial-service whatever. Back in the woods, several miles from the harbor the body was borne on a common truck, and buried, with a rude mound to mark the spot, and a stake driven down at the head instead of a tombstone.

Such was the amount of respect shown to our common humanity! Such the measure of sympathy and reflection drawn forth by this awful calamity! But there was a very small number of humane, tender souls, amid the reckless, unreflecting mass, who though they might not interfere with the general management of the matter, recalled the tender musings of an English poet—

"Who was her father? who was her mother?

Had she a sister? had she a brother?"

And with these words sprang up a world of thought and sympathy, which cannot be drawn out upon paper, which cannot be coined into words. And there were young hearts that felt, and young eyes that wept, at this first sight of death and the grave.

CHAPTER IX.

A Happy Discovery.

R. Williams was fully installed as chief engineer at the harbor, and as speedily as possible was becoming settled. He had rented a house, had fitted it up, and was expecting his wife and three little children by the next trip of "The Northern Light." Meanwhile, his home was at Sandy's.

It was near the close of the first day after the funeral; and, from the uncongenial society of the place, the recent catastrophe, and the absence of his family, he was feeling quite sad and lonely. As he went out of the house, after his evening meal, he wandered round the beach to the farthest part of the point. Here he was quite out of sight of the village. Behind him, and away to his right, was the shore,—a great bed of limestone, broken into all shapes and sizes, now level like a rude highway, and now rising abruptly like an irregular wall. Beyond this was the forest, of meagre growth, and of a cold, dark green. Directly before him, and away to the left as far as the eye could reach, was the lake, its waters stirred by a fresh evening breeze, and breaking in gentle waves at his feet. The sun was just touching the horizon, and, like a great orb of flame, seemed about to dip into the distant waters. It cast a stream of light across the lake, which grew more intense in the distance, like the path of the just, that shineth more and more unto the perfect day. Clouds, transfigured into golden, crimson, and purple light, rose about the setting sun like the gates of Paradise.

90

Mr. Williams had an eye for the beautiful in nature, and a heart that responded in sublime and tender meditations. He seated himself upon a rock, and gazed devoutly upon the scene before him.

Presently he was startled with the sound of footsteps upon the loose stones of the shore. On looking up, he saw Harry, who untaught in the nicer points of good manners and overborne by an ardent desire to open the secret of his heart to one whom, he somehow felt, would sympathize with him, had hesitatingly followed him to his retreat.

The child halted a moment when he met Mr. Williams's eye, and seemed quite confused, as if not knowing how to account for himself. But there was something in his look, half of bashfulness, half of longing, that set Mr. Williams on the right track.

"Come here, Harry, my boy," said he with a smile, and stretching out his hand towards him: "come, sit down by me on this rock."

Very modestly, Harry took his seat by Mr.

Williams without saying a word.

"Did you want to speak to me about something, Harry?" he asked very kindly.

Harry made no reply; but the tremor of his lip, and the bright tear in his eye, were more eloquent to Mr. Williams than words.

"Is there a burden on your heart, my boy?" he continued, full well convinced as to the child's trouble.

Harry's heart overflowed. Turning his face away, he wept with that free outgushing of sorrow which only a child knows.

Mr. Williams's sympathies were thoroughly roused. Throwing his arms around Harry, he wept with him.

"I think I know your trouble, Harry," said Mr. Williams, when his feelings had so subsided that he could speak. "There is a great weight on your heart. You feel that your heart is wicked; that your life has been wicked; that unless you are somehow made better, you cannot live happily, nor die in peace. Isn't that it?"

Harry nodded his head in ascent, accompanying it with one of those hearty sobs common to children after hard weeping. Mr. Williams had stated the matter more clearly than it had been defined in Harry's thoughts, but, somehow, the words suited his feelings.

As soon as Harry was calm enough, he told Mr. Williams how his religious interest first began: how he had met a stranger at the dock, who had told him about Jesus, and our need of him; how he had thought of it ever since.

"I try hard, but I can't git good," said the child artlessly. "When I go to bed in the night, I think how bad I have been all day. That makes me cry, and promise God to do right all day if he'll give me one day more. But, the next night, I find I am as bad as ever. So I haven't been good yet. Sometimes I feel so wicked, I almost wish there wasn't any God,—that we could get along just as well without him. But then we can't, and I'm bad to think of it."

"No, no, Harry: we can't do without God. He is our best friend," said Mr. Williams very earnestly. "There, do you know what that means?" he continued, holding Harry's thumb on his little fat wrist. "That's from the beating of your heart, which keeps you alive. God makes your heart beat every time. He gives you every breath."

"He made me,—the man told me," added Harry, referring to the stranger who had first instructed him in these things.

"Yes; and he keeps us alive every minute. He puts the color on your cheek, and the brightness in your eye. If it were not for him, that sun would never rise again," said Mr. Williams, pointing to the gorgeous clouds which closed about the place of sunset. "And he has given his only Son to die for us that he might take away all our sins, and give

94

us new hearts, so that we can do right."

"Tell me about that," urged Harry, who was eager to hear the story over, which the stranger had told him long before.

"The Son of God came down to this world, more than eighteen hundred years ago, and became a little babe. He was not born in a great and beautiful house, but in a stable, and was put in a manger for a cradle, for his parents were poor. He grew up like other little boys around him, and, no doubt, played with them; but he must have been a great deal better than any other little child, for he never sinned in all his life. Wouldn't you like to have been one of the little boys that played with him, so as to have had him for your friend?"

Harry nodded his head with much interest.

"As he was poor," continued Mr. Williams, "he worked for a living. Was a carpenter, and, no doubt, did many a hard day's work. When he was about thirty years old, the heavenly father called him from his business, and he went about doing good. Great crowds of people gathered about him everywhere, and followed him from place to place, bringing their sick and their dying friends to be blessed by him. As he was the Son of God, and had all power, he put his fingers on the eyes of the blind and made them see. He took sick people by the hand, and raised them from their beds, and they were cured: even the dead he raised to life again, by simply speaking to them; while poor, weak women only touched his clothes and were made well. One time they brought little children to him, and he took them in his arms and blessed them. By and by, wicked men put him to death. They took him in the night, while he was out in the field praying. They took off his clothes from his back, and whipped him with a great whip of many lashes, each lash having a piece of bone or iron fastened to the end, so that it might sink into his flesh. They whipped him till his back was all torn and bleeding: then they tied sharp thorns around his head, so that they pressed into his forehead and temples; and they mocked him, spit in his face, and struck him on the cheek with their hands. Putting upon his back, all bleeding and torn, a heavy cross of wood,—heavy enough for a well, strong man to carry,—they led him away to put him to death, a great crowd of wicked people following after and crying out, 'Away with him! let him be killed!' They came to a terrible place! one where the wickedest people in all the country were put to death, by being nailed to a wooden cross, and left hanging in the scorching sun by day and the damp cold of night, till they perished, or some beast devoured them. Here they drove great nails through the hands and feet of Jesus, and nailed him to the cross. He died amidst the most terrible suffering. Then his body was begged by his friends, who took him down and buried him. After three days, he rose from the dead, and ascended up to heaven. There he hears our prayers, and helps us for the sake of his own sufferings and death. All this he does for you, Harry!"

"What can I do for him?" earnestly inquired Harry.

"You can love him and trust in him," answered Mr. Williams.

"I want to: I hope I'll know how," continued the child, so simply, so sincerely, that Mr. Williams was reminded of the man who said to Jesus, when on earth, "I believe: help thou mine unbelief."

"I will tell you a story," said he to Harry. "Perhaps it will help you to see what Jesus wants you to do. Once a little boy was playing about on the top of a very high building, that was just being built, it had a great many loose boards lying about its top, and timbers and stone around it below. As he skipped about carelessly, he stepped on a loose board, which gave way, and he fell. As he fell he caught the end of a rope which hung over the side

98

of the building. There he hung, high up in the air. It was hard to hold on. His arms and hands ached. But he knew, if he let go the rope, he would be dashed in pieces on the rocks beneath him. Just as his strength was failing, and it seemed he could not hold on another moment, a man ran to his rescue, and, stretching out his strong arms directly below him, cried out, 'Let go the rope, my boy, and drop into my arms. Don't be afraid. I'll save you!' The boy dropped into his arms, and was saved. Just so you are hanging over the place of destruction. Just so Jesus comes to you, his heart full of love and pity, and, stretching out his strong arms, calls on you to drop into them and be saved."

"Only that!—nothing more?" exclaimed Harry, his large clear blue eyes overflowing with astonishment. Could it be that Jesus required so little of him!—only to trust?

"Only that!—Nothing more!" repeated Mr. Williams with emphasis, as he gazed fully and

earnestly into the fair young face turned up to him.

A new light began to dawn on Harry. Now he had learned, not only of God, but of God in Christ,—a Being who knew all his feelings and struggles, who loved and pitied him, and gave his life to save him. He felt that he could trust him and was happier than he had been for many days. The day had deepened into twilight, and twilight into darkness. Upon the rocky shore, amidst the solemn sound of the waves which broke softly at their side, Mr. Williams and Harry knelt and prayed together.

Mr. Williams held Harry's hand with a firm tender grasp, as they walked homeward over their rough and stony path. And this path might represent another, which Harry, with his hand in his Savior's, and a new fountain of love springing up in his heart, was treading with an easier, firmer step. Mr. Williams was silently rejoicing over his new discovery. Like Elijah of old, who thought himself alone amidst the worshippers of Baal, he had supposed himself far separate from all Christian sympathies; but even here he had found one of Christ's little ones. That was like a star of hope to him. Was it not the sign of better days for this famishing region?

CHAPTER X.

Night Thoughts.

MR. Williams retired at an early hour as usual, but not to sleep. Hour after hour he lay absorbed in exciting meditations. The deep quiet throughout the house, unbroken, save by the heavy breathing common to sound sleep, and the loud tick of the old clock, with its still louder tolling of the passing hour, convinced him, that, of the household, he was alone in his wakefulness. The harbor, too, was all quiet excepting the occasional pattering of rain upon the roof, the roar of the furnace-flames, and the breaking of the surf on the beach. He resorted to every method to drive away his thoughts. He counted, repeated to himself hymns and paragraphs of Scripture, then went over the same backwards; but midnight came, and several hours after, before "tired Nature's sweet restorer" came to his relief.

He thought of Harry, and wondered that he had not before spoken to him, personally, about the matter that rested so heavily upon his heart. The thought came to him with power, that there might be many little ones, who carried about those daily longings for spiritual life, without any one to speak the first word, and thus break the tempter's spell, that binds the human heart, and keeps it dumb on the most important of all human interests. If so, how great would be the responsibility of those to whose influence was given the tenderness of young life!

Then he reviewed the dreadful scene of the late

catastrophe, and could but regard it as an indication of the moral condition of the community about him,—an outcropping of the corruption and wretchedness of its inner life. He thought of the varied and strange providences that had broken up his former situation in business, and driven him by necessity to this moral waste. Was it a mere question of the necessaries of life,—of bread and butter for his wife and children. Above this, had he not a mission here? He thought of Paul, when, in his second great missionary tour, he lay down to sleep across the sea from the Macedonian shores, his heart full of sorrow over the darkness of heathenism, and saw a Macedonian at his bedside, crying "Come over and help us!" and in the person of Harry, whose tears and cries were still in his heart, Mr. Williams seemed to meet the same appeal, in behalf of the benighted region about him.

His deepest soul responded to the appeal; but oh, his weakness! his inefficiency! He rose, and silently, with tears, consecrated himself to the work which Providence had evidently placed before him. It was a solemn and delightful moment. He arose strengthened; for every consecrated man is strong, having first felt his own weakness, and then having been anointed with power from on high.

The few hours' sleep which followed were very refreshing, and Mr. Williams rose to a new life.

CHAPTER XI.

A New Enterprise.

HE morning sun rose clear and beautiful, after a night of summer showers. Every rock and cliff stood forth in brighter colors; trees and flowers, newly washed, glistened in drops of pearl; a fresh breeze from off the land was redolent from the hills, and the very earth seemed to give forth a fragrance. The sky was deep, with scarce a cloud, and the azure seemed brighter and richer, as if the showers had washed out the very heavens; while the sun beams sparkled and danced upon the waters, not yet quieted from the winds of the night.

When Harry waked, the sunlight was streaming

in through the little window which lighted the small garret making the boy's sleeping apartment. He had slept soundly, and, seemingly, after the usual time; for his brothers were up and gone, and he heard the sound of business about the village.

He scarcely knew what to think of himself. He seemed to have waked up into a new life. Oh, the sweet peace that filled his heart! the joy that welled up into all his being, and overflowed in tears of rapture! He thought of the weight that had rested so heavily upon him; but it was altogether gone. He had no fear of death now, nor of the Judgment. God was no longer a terror to him, but the object of a new and tender love.

He sprang up and dressed himself, and prayed as he had never prayed before. He thanked God out of a heart full and overflowing; and his petitions were no longer addressed as to one afar off,—one who was scarcely any thing like personal reality to him,—but to the Christ, glorious and divine, yet stretching out to him a human hand, having a human heart that loved and pitied, and an ear to hear his cry, as his mother would hear him when he called for bread. Nor let any one think such knowledge too wonderful for a child like him; for, though there is much in the mysterious personage of the God-man that not even the wisest can fathom, there is also much with which even such little ones can sympathize.

Harry came tripping down stairs with even a lighter step than usual; so much so, that his mother, absorbed in her breakfast preparation, was startled, and, straightened herself up from over her frying-pan, looked upon him with a look of wonder.

The child could scarcely contain his secret. He wanted to tell some one how happy he was, how near Jesus seemed to him, and how he loved him. How natural, too, that he should want to tell his mother! But he had not been brought up so close to his mother's heart as many children are. She loved her bright-eyed Harry, whose merry, musical laugh, and genial overflow of joyous young life, stole about her heart like rays of sunshine forcing their way through her cloudy sky; but she knew nothing of that delicately refined affection which takes a child into the holy of holies of the heart's sanctuary, and keeps open door between the secrets that dwell in the breast of parent and child.

Harry went out upon the dock, and, sitting upon a pile of lumber, gazed upon the beautiful world about him. Could it be that those rocks and cliffs had always been just as they were on that happy morning? Was not the great wall, running along the main land on the opposite side of the harbor, much higher and more grand than ever before? Oh, the lake, the sky, the sun! Surely, they had never been so brilliant, so glorious!

Every little thing in nature had a new interest to him, and he discovered a new love for every object that God has made. The fish that bent like a bow above the water in search of his breakfast, the white kittens that played and frolicked about the dock, the robin that sung in the evergreen near by, all made him happy; and the very roar of the furnace seemed like a grand chord in nature's harmony.

True, he did not reflect on all this with the accuracy and profoundness of those who are older and can boast of culture in the fine arts, and long experience in the observation of nature; but so simple and benevolent are the beauties and grandeur of the world which God has spread out before us, that even a child may read with delight.

When breakfast came, Mr. Williams did not fail to see the new face that Harry wore. "The child's heart has found rest," he said to himself, as he looked upon him so fresh and radiant, like a rose on a June morning: "God be gracious to him!" Scarcely less happy was Mr. Williams himself. The morning had been new to him, after his night of reflection and new resolutions; and a careful observer might have seen new joy and peace on his countenance.

"Come to the shop with me," said he to Harry, after breakfast.

Harry was glad to go; for he felt a new love for Mr. Williams, and wanted to tell him what a change he had met.

"You are very happy this morning,—are you not, Harry?" said Mr. Williams, as soon as he was fairly at work in his shop.

Harry nodded his head emphatically, and smiled the happiest smile Mr. Williams had seen for many a day.

"I have something new to tell you," continued Mr. Williams. "We shall have a Sunday school here at the harbor."

"What's that?" inquired Harry, with much curiosity.

He had never heard of a school of any kind. The

word had no possible meaning to him.

"It is for boys and girls to come together to learn about God, about Jesus, and how to do right."

"I'll go," promised Harry, pleased with such a prospect.

"I thought a great deal about this last night. This morning I have been round bright and early, inquiring into things. Two families of good people, who love Jesus, have just moved here. One lives a mile back in the woods, at the coal-pits. The other up here, in the large brown house in the middle of the row. He will open his house for the school, and we will begin next Sunday."

"I'm glad. I'll go round and git the boys and girls to come."

"That's just the thing for you to do, Harry. Work for Jesus in that way, and you will continue to be happy, and grow better every day. My little boy, Frank, is about as large as you; and Clara, my little daughter, is some larger. By the next trip of

"The Northern Light," they will be here; and they will be delighted to go with you, and help you."

"How will it be?—the—the—what did you call it?" queried Harry, delighted with the design of the new enterprise, and wishing to know something of its method.

"The Sunday school?"

"Yes,—yes!"

"We shall have books to learn from. We shall have singing too," continued Mr. Williams.

All the singing Harry had ever heard was a rude rendering of vulgar rhymes. He wondered if the singing that Mr. Williams referred to could be anything like that.

"Now go and play, Harry," said Mr. Williams kindly; "and this afternoon, when the boat comes in, be on hand. I'll introduce you to my little ones."

Harry bounded away, and, casting many an eager look across the water, found the hours long till the boat appeared.

CHAPTER XII.

Out in the Highways.

"T HE Northern Light" had landed Mr. Williams's family; and Harry had received his introduction to Frank and Clara, who were neater and more interesting than any children he had ever seen.

There was no time to be lost in the Sunday-school project; so, on the first morning after their arrival, Harry's young friends started out with him into the highways to canvass for it.

According to Mr. Williams's advice, they began at head-quarters. Mr. Alton was *the* man of the place. He had the entire oversight of every department of the business, and all the employees looked up to him as a sort of king of the harbor. He had never manifested any sentiment whatever as to religion; but he was a so-called moral man, and had a very sweet little girl, whom he might wish to have in the Sunday school; and, if his endorsement of the enterprise could be gained, it would be of great value in the community.

The little company of missionaries went up the steep bank of the point, to the large white house; and Harry rang the bell, feeling rather timid, for he had never ventured so near the grandest house at the harbor before, and Mr. Alton had always been disposed to deal in short measure with the rude flock of children of the place. But he knew his was a noble cause, and he nerved himself up to all the courage possible.

Mrs. Alton came to the door, and very kindly invited them in.

Harry, being somewhat known, had agreed to be

spokesman. So, as soon as they were fairly seated, he opened up their errand.

"These is Frank and Clara Williams," he said, with natural politeness, to the elegant lady of the house. "They've just come here to live."

"I'm very glad to see them," added Mrs. Alton, as Harry hesitated in trying to bring forward his errand, in connection with the young strangers just introduced. "I hope more such bright and interesting boys and girls may come to the harbor."

"Mr. Williams—their father—is going to get up a—a Sunday school at Mr. Hawley's. It's goin' to begin next Sunday; and we've come to see if your little girl can go."

"That is all very kind, and, perhaps, very well," complimented the lady, out of politeness rather than for any particular regard for religion. "Kittie used to go to Sunday school before we came here: I don't know what she'll think of it now."

"Oh ma, I want to go! I love Sunday school so

116

much!" spoke up Kittie, as she came into the room, overhearing what her mother had just said.

"This is my Kittie," said Mrs. Alton, introducing a spritely little girl of about eight years, bright blue-eyed, rosy-cheeked, and having such a profusion of yellow curls, that her plump shoulders and full forehead were half-buried in their soft, silken tresses.

"Is it a Sunday school I hears you talkin' 'bout?" inquired a tall, fat colored woman who came in from an adjoining room, where she happened to catch a part of the conversation.

"Yes, Toodie: you'll be glad to learn about it," replied Mrs. Alton. "You're so fond of such things."

"A Sunday school in dis ar place! Bress de Lord!" exclaimed Toodie, as she stood in the middle of the floor, lifting up her plump, black hand in astonishment. "I's been 'fraid dis ar place so near de heathen, dat we'd neber git anything o'dat sort

117

in my time."

"Tell your good man I'll be on hand," she continued as she started to leave the room. "What's de
time, do you say?"

"Half-past ten in the forenoon," answered
Harry, who knew Mr. Williams would be glad to
hear of another helper in the good work.

"You'll take me, Toodie, if ma'll let me go,—
won't you?" pleaded Kittie.

"Yes, indeed! bress you, my honey. "I'll go
laughin' all de way, if mammy 'll let you go."

"Well, I guess we must let Kittie go," consented
Mrs. Alton playfully. "You may expect them bright
and early next Sunday."

The errand was done, and the object accom-
plished, and our little friends rose to leave. Just as
they were going out of the door they met Miss
Elliott, Mrs. Dr. Sprague's sister. Before she had
got fairly in, or the young visitors fairly out, Kittie
had announced the Sunday school, with the utmost

118

enthusiasm.

"Indeed! A Sunday school!" exclaimed the pious young lady. "That's delightful news."

"Tell Mr. Williams he may count me for one in the good work," she pledged, on learning the facts of the case.

"Haven't we done well?" said Clara, delighted with their success, as the little trio tripped down the steep bank into the street.

"Hope we'll do as well everywhere," added Harry.

"But we mustn't be discouraged if we don't," cautioned Frank. "It's a great work; and pa says the people here are very wicked, so they may not like such good things right away."

"Where shall we go next?" inquired Clara.

"To Mr. Henry's," answered Harry. "He's got the most children of anyone in town,—four boys and five girls."

Mr. Henry was foreman at the furnace. He had

always lived in the mining regions, and had scarcely been inside of a church in his life. Of course his children had never been in Sunday school, and he himself scarcely knew what such a thing meant. But he was naturally generous and obliging, and might put his family under the care of so good a man as Mr. Williams, out of sheer accommodation.

With his wife the case might be less hopeful. While she had had no advantages above her husband, and, consequently, was no better able to appreciate a good institution in society, she lacked his kindness and generosity. But her large, ill-bred, noisy family was a great pest to her; and she was glad, at any time, to be rid of them a single hour.

They lived in the first of the long row of brown houses, which our young friends came to on their way from Mr. Alton's; and so loud was the uproar made by the large family of children, turned loose on the uncarpeted floor, that Harry knocked quite loudly and several times, before he could make himself heard.

"Come in," shrieked out Mrs. Henry, above the rattle and clatter of chairs, benches, and tables, and in no very good-natured tone.

The commotion subsided as the visitors entered; and, as they seated themselves upon a long bench near the door, they had the benefit of a thorough scanning, from head to foot, by Mrs. Henry and the family in general. Clara's tall, slender figure, full, black eyes, and dark, wavy hair, and more particularly her gentleness and lady-like manner, were carefully noted; and Frank, short, plump, rosy-cheeked, and so full of life and good-humor that it sparkled in his clear blue eyes, flowed over every feature of his round face, and turned the very hairs of his head into frolicsome twists and curls, was no less an object of interest.

"These is some of the new folks jest come, I s'pose?" said Mrs. Henry, standing in the middle of the floor, with a broom in one hand and biting the finger-nails of the other.

"Clara and Frank are," responded Harry. "I'm Harry Sandy, and lived here before the town was built. Mr. Williams,—Clara and Frank's father, is goin' to begin a Sunday school at Mr. Hawley's, next Sunday mornin'—half-past ten. Please, ma'am, he'd like to have your children come."

"What did you say it was, boy, eh?" queried Mrs. Henry, in a loud tone, and with a puzzled air.

"A Sunday school," added Harry.

"What's that for?"

"To learn out of the Bible," joined Clara. "To learn about God, and how to serve him."

"Humph! Well, that won't do 'em no hurt, I reckon," said the curious woman; "and it 'ill do me good to git 'em out o' the way a while. I'll agree. But ask their father. He's at the furnace. He knows more about sich things than I do, maybe."

Clara and Frank were quite ready to go to the furnace. Their father had written them a great deal

122

about it before they came to the harbor, and they had not yet visited it. So they started at once to see Mr. Henry.

They found him busy preparing to draw off the melted iron. After the furnace was drained, and its contents of fiery liquid run into moulds in the sand, to cool and harden for shipping, he would be able to listen to what they had to say.

Meanwhile, the young strangers were pleased to look on, and see how all this was done. They observed the large bed of brown sand, gradually sloping from the mouth of the furnace at one end of the large building, and extending to the other end. This sand was carefully smoothed over, and mould- ed into long rows of gutters, into which the melted iron was run, and formed into large, straight pieces, called pigs.

Mr. Henry was giving orders to the men, who punched open the mouth of the furnace, which was stopped up with a kind of clay, and let off the scum of the melted iron, called cinder. When it first flowed out, it looked like a stream of fire; but it soon cooled off, and turned almost as white as snow. It was full of pores, and very brittle; and, when held to the ear, was full of crackling sounds. Some pieces of it were solid, and looked like glass of different colors.

After the cinder, the iron was drawn off. It ran along the gutters in the sand, like oil, and was about the color of a bright flame. It gave off an immense heat while cooling, and it was several hours before it could be handled.

Clara and Frank were highly pleased with the business, but they were shocked at the profanity of the workmen; for when they punched open the furnace, and particles of melted iron, glowing with a white heat, occasionally flew in every direction, burning their clothing, and sometimes their flesh, there was a volley of oaths that was perfectly terrible. The strong men, who carried out the iron after it was moulded into pigs, occasionally scratching or cutting themselves with the sharp corners and edges, used the name of Christ so shockingly that Clara turned pale, and Frank felt his very blood chill.

During the hurry and bustle of drawing off the furnace, Harry had kept his eye on the tall, fat, rosy-faced man, known by every man and child in the village as good-natured, jolly Mr. Henry. Nor had the trim little company failed to get an occasional look from him, even before they ventured to speak to him. Rough and uncouth as he was, he had an eye for pretty children. He admired them as he would a pretty flower or a bright star; and was more than once heard to say, that, in all the wide world, he did not believe there was any thing so charming as their bright eyes and rosy cheeks.

He received our young friends with a real kindness, that cheered them on in their good work, and very readily promised the patronage of his family.

"You've jest made the hit in comin' here," said he. "Half a dozen men or more in this establishment have little fellows at home. I guess they'll all send. S'pose you wouldn't mind havin' little good company like mine, eh? I might go round with you, and see 'em."

"Thank you, sir," said Clara politely: "thank you. That will help ever so much."

Mr. Henry was just the pilot needed in this large establishment. Every item of interest was carefully pointed out, and accompanied with an overflow of pleasantry and quaint remarks, that heightened satisfaction at every turn; and he knew the men as a sailor knows his boat, or a farmer his horses, and could approach them to the best advantage.

On they went, into the large department where great stacks of coal and ore were housed, where was a powerful and noisy crushing machine, grinding down the large chunks of ore for the furnace; into the engine-room, where was a huge steam-power, which served the machinery throughout the establishment, and plied an immense bellows, operating at the base of the furnace-shaft to intensify the heat.

When they had canvassed all the lower part of the building with good success,—that is to say, with fair promises,—Mr. Henry proposed to call on the fireman in the highest story, who fed the huge shaft from the top.

This point was accessible by a long, dark, winding stairway, rising some sixty feet; but their guide proposed to our young friends to ascend on the large elevator, which carried up the coal and ore. The ride was so romantic, that the boys laughed outright; but Clara was a little nervous, and would have been dizzy, had it not been for the strong man who steadied her.

"The finest cargo you ever took up here, Sam!" exclaimed Mr. Henry to the fireman, as they landed on the highest story.

"Sam, here, has got a whole tribe of little chaps. He'll be in for the school."

Sam listened very attentively to the report of the Sunday-school plan, and promised to send his whole family of boys, if they could get up clothes that were decent.

"No need of bein' proud in this, Sam," said Mr. Henry. "It isn't for makin' show."

The great shaft, full sixty feet high, and many feet in diameter, which rolled up its huge bulk of flame far above its top, loading the air with a heavy cloud of black smoke, was an interesting affair, as explained by Mr. Henry. It was kept full of coal and ore, from top to bottom. This was a solid mass of fire, furnished with a thorough draft below, and the great bellows already referred to. The gas generated by burning the coal was conducted back to the base of the shaft, and turned into the immense column of fire to increase its intensity.

"That's about the hottest fire that can be got

up," said Mr. Henry.

It made Clara think of the place "where the worm dieth not, and the fire is not quenched."

The company descended by the elevator, and having finished their errand, and thanked Mr. Henry for his kindness, hurried home to dinner, to resume their work again in the afternoon.

The afternoon, however, was not so encouraging. Now they came in contact with a more unpromising part of the community. The better class of inhabitants had been solicited in the forenoon; and the work that remained was nearly confined to the log-houses on Shanty Street, which were occupied, for the most part, by a low grade of German, French, and Irish.

Clara had scarcely seen any thing so revolting in the worst parts of the city of Cleveland. The huts were built on the very edge of the street. In front and around them, hens scratched, and hogs wallowed in the mire. These domesticated creatures

129

were thrown into great excitement by the new visitors. The poultry set up a regular concert of cackling, and the swine grunted and snorted as if taking alarm. Frank was vain enough to wonder if it were not because of the rare appearance of decent-appearing people in those parts. Oh, the stench that met them on every hand! and the filthy, ragged children! Clara almost wondered if they could be a part of common humanity.

They called at every house, with scarcely any success. No: they omitted one. When they came in front of Pat Sharky's, they met Pat sneaking out, with a look not unlike that of a dog with his tail between his legs; while Madam Sharky, the tallest, fattest woman in the village, stood in the door, her eyes flashing with anger, and her face red with excitement, as she held a broomstick in one hand, and doubled the other into a huge fist, which she shook most significantly, as she followed Pat with a torrent of vulgar eloquence, quite unfit to be recorded here.

Of course the children excused themselves, for the time at least, from calling here, and passed on to the uninviting homes beyond.

On all the rest of the street, their reception was very cool. It might be well expressed in the response given their invitation by Mrs. Flannigan, who lived in the last hut in the street:—

"An' sure an' what de ye think the praste would be afther doin' to me, if he caught me afther the like o' that! No: niver, niver in all my born days!"

Our young friends had done a large day's work, and returned home somewhat fatigued; but they had never felt happier in their life, for they had been about their Master's business. That was the first day's work ever done for the cause of religion at the harbor. The next Sabbath would tell how much of an impression had been made.

CHAPTER XIII.

The Sunday School.

HE tour of the young missionaries created quite an excitement. The Sunday school proposed was so entirely new, so unheard-of to most of the inhabitants, that they looked forward to it with much curiosity. Fathers and mothers wondered what it would be like, and children were as full of marvel as if they had been expecting a show. The subject was talked about and discussed, and the time seemed long till Sunday came.

Saturday night brought a storm. Till on into the morning, lightenings gleamed and flashed, and thunders rattled and roared as if the very elements were at war. Rain fell in torrents; and the lake, lashed into fury, rolled its troubled waters noisily upon the shore.

After a night of unrefreshing sleep, the dawn came with a gray and feeble light, that was long struggling into day. The storm had ceased; but, for hours, dark clouds floated low under the whole sky, and a gray fog hung in heavy folds about the cliffs, and reconnoitered in the harbor.

"Do you think the rain is over, Pa? I'd had hoped we should have a fine day!" said Clara Williams, as she rose at a very early hour, quite pale after her restless night, and looking very much disappointed.

"I do not know enough about this climate my daughter, to tell," replied her father. "But we must not be anxious. Who is it that takes care of the storms and the sunshine?"

Clara's eye brightened as a new train of thought came to her relief. Why should she trouble herself about the weather? Did not her heavenly Father hold the winds in the hollow of his hand? Were not cloud and sunshine alike at his bidding?—and he loved Sunday schools more than she did.

But trust in Providence, and prayer for what we feel we need, are not inconsistent. So Clara stole away to her chamber, and prayed for God to drive away the clouds, and give the people of the harbor sunshine for their Sunday school.

She almost clapped her hands for joy a few hours afterward, when she saw a bright spot of blue sky peering through the clouds, and then, gradually, the whole army of cloud-banks and fogs driven out across the water, before a fresh wind from off the hills. Long before the time for Sunday school, the sun was shining with a brightness that made Nature glisten in her newly washed robes, and warmed the very hills into fragrance.

Full half an hour before the time of Sunday school, the children were on their way. Almost every one went to the window to see the new and beautiful sight. Before, Sunday, to the children, had scarcely differed from other days. If they were washed and dressed a little cleaner than usual, the day had barely begun when they were as thoroughly covered with iron-rust or coal-smut as on any other day of the week; and they had never known any higher employment or its hallowed hours than their common romp and rolic. To-day their clothes continued perfectly clean; the wildest, roughest boys in the village walked with quiet and dignity of gentlemen; boisterous voices were subdued to sweetness; hard, cold features softened into kindness. The people hardly knew the children of their own town, so great was the change wrought by cleanliness, and the first step towards good order.

The place of meeting, with its little audience,

was somewhat romantic. The room, which was of middling dimensions, was exceedingly plain. No carpet, no pictures, but little furniture, and that the very commonest, no paper on the walls,—they were clean and white as new-fallen snow. The brown doors had neither finger-mark nor speck; the windows were clear and transparent as the air itself; the floor was so scrubbed into whiteness that one might have eaten his dinner from off it with a good stomach.

Mr. Hawley evidently had looked forward to the work with faith. He had expected a full house, and made his preparations accordingly. Boards had been carried in, and so adjusted that the room could be seated to its utmost capacity.

Would not God recognize this confidence in the success of effort put forth for the truth? Would he not say as to one of old, "According to thy faith so be it unto thee"? Mr. Hawley was not disappointed. Almost every seat was occupied.

The gathering contained a great variety. There were the Williamses and Miss Elliott, neat and tasty enough to be in keeping with any audience; Kittie Alton and the young Sandys, fresh and beautiful as morning flowers. The little Henrys, the Reilys, and the Richardsons, in full rustic hardiness and simplicity; plump, black, shiny Toodie, decked out in purest white muslin, and white-straw hat all a-bloom with artificials. Andy, her husband,—a hardy, stalwart African, full six feet three who worked among the coal-pits back in the wood,—had heard of the Sunday school, and, being an earnest, pure-hearted Christian, was on hand to bear his part in the enterprise.

But the matter was not all romance. However skillful the workmen, it is difficult to work without tools. Herein Mr. Williams was exceedingly deficient. There was no library of elegant books, no charming papers, and but few able to read them if there had been; no singing-books, and hardly any one able to sing. A few, who could read, had brought Bibles and Testaments. These were the full amount of appliances for the great work.

Of course, Mr. Williams was chosen superintendent; and now came the tug of war, the test of generalship. But the good man had *the grand* qualification,—*"faith."* Why should he be faint-hearted? Was not the same One who commanded the disciples of old to feed the multitude of thousands with five loaves and two small fishes, saying to him, "Give ye them to eat?" The twelve baskets of fragments taken up proved that obligation may transcend the means in hand, and that he who labors for God may not calculate results from apparent causes.

First, the superintendent led in singing a hymn, which he gave out a few lines at a time, repeating it and singing it over till nearly all could join in. Then he read the Word of God and prayed. While he prayed, all knelt down, and silently repeated each petition after him.

The classes were arranged. There was employ-ment for each one able to teach, Andy and Toodie not excepted.

Seldom have teachers addressed themselves to their work with such thorough and well-directed zeal. They would not merely be regular in their attendance on Sabbath, making good preparation for their work; but they would take a personal, prayerful interest in each scholar, holding the same relation to the little flock that a pastor should to his church and congregation.

The exercise was not a mere entertainment,—it was true spiritual worship. Hearts were awed as in the presence of God, and carried away a deep and solemn impression. There had been a successful beginning of great work; and the band of workers returned home with enlarged hearts and increasing faith of God.

CHAPTER XIV.

The Minister.

THE community at the harbor was rapidly growing in business and in population. A second smelting-stack was going up; and teams, coal-pits, tugs, scows, workmen, and every other accompaniment of the main business, were increasing accordingly. The land cleared in procuring wood for the coal-pits was worked by farmers, and lumber-mills were going up at several points in the vicinity.

The growing importance of the place started

new points of business apart from that of the iron company. A small art-gallery was set up, a life-insurance agent put out his sign, and the government surveyor for the county took quarters in one of the houses belonging to the company.

The vitality and increase of business at this point stimulated the growth of settlements adjoining, and these re-acted in promoting the prosperity of the harbor. Very soon here would be a county-seat.

Mr. Williams was a man who went through the world wide-awake, and he brought the first-fruits of his enterprise to the cause of religion. He saw that the harbor was to have a future, and he was anxious that the entire region should be consecrated to God. For this he prayed and thought and labored.

Already his Sunday school—less than a month old—had become a power. By constant perseverance, nearly every child in the village had been gathered in; and, for several miles around, families of farmers and workmen, in the forest and among the coal-pits, were being brought under its influence.

We are justifiable in speaking of the *influence* of this Sunday school; for it had positive, moral and religious power. The teachers' hearts were filled with love, which drew the children to them as a magnet draws iron; and the scriptures were so thoroughly studied, and so elaborately and fascinatingly taught, that the young hearts were thrilled with interest, and so completely saturated with the lesson that they carried it about with them all the week. The instructions were not such as might be given by more educational teachers,—not critical or learned, but simple, practical, and earnest, such as were wrought out by the true Christian experience. Hence their power over the heart and light.

Any one might observe a gradual change in the children. There was less swearing among the boys, fewer blackened eyes and bloody noses, less of general depredation about the village, and more obedience to parents at home. Mr. Henry declared, that it would be well to invest money in so good a cause as the Sunday school, and even Sandy thought it a paying institution. Nor did it fail to affect the older part of the community. Somehow, in a subtle way, a good influence was abroad. Parents grew more loving and spoke more kindly to the little ones; and a daily contact with the truths of Scripture through these warm, tender, young natures, was acting upon the very springs of their life.

Mr. Williams saw that here was a field white for the harvest; and, after much thought and prayer, he consulted the little praying-circle as to procuring a minister of the gospel. There could be but one opinion concerning the want of the community; but how could a preacher be supported? Mr. Williams was a practical man, and looked the question fairly in the face, with that faith before which mountains of difficulty flee away,—a faith that works!

There were now five Christian families at the harbor; none of them wealthy, but all comfortable. If they would give one tenth of their income, according to Scripture, half the support of a minister would be secured. Then there were friends who would aid. Dr. Sprague had already offered to be responsible for forty dollars a year, if a good preacher could be found. Besides, Mr. Williams stood ready to give even more than a tenth of his income, if necessary.

Correspondence was had with a personal acquaintance of Mr. Williams, who seemed as he thought, especially adapted to the field, and very soon he was landed by "The Northern Light."

Mr. Williams was on hand to receive him, and his coming made quite a sensation in the village. He had been expected and talked about, and for the most part, seemed welcome.

Many of the Sunday-school children were on the dock, and gazed, with curious reverence upon the tall, genteel personage in black, who looked around with a look that seemed to say, "I love you all, and want to do you good."

"How the place has grown since I was here!" said the preacher, as he went up from the dock towards the row of brown houses with Mr. Williams.

"Since you were here?" queried Mr. Williams.

"Yes: I forgot to state, in my note, that I had some knowledge of the place. I was here and spent the greater part of a day, soon after the iron company began their enterprise; came over on a tug from Escanaba, and loitered and fished in the sunshine."

Mr. Williams thought of Harry's account of the stranger who had so wonderfully instructed him, and wondered if the new-comer could be he.

"I remember that log-house," continued the stranger, pointing towards Sandy's dwelling, "and a little lad, poor fellow, bright and beautiful as any child I have ever seen, but wholly uninstructed."

"Harry Sandy!" exclaimed Mr. Williams. "Here he comes!"

Harry was on his way to the steamer at the dock, as fast as his nimble feet could carry him, but halted suddenly on meeting Mr. Williams, and looked at the stranger with a happy look of recognition.

"This is my boy!" exclaimed the new-comer, stepping up to the lad, and taking both his fat hands in his. "Do you know me, Harry?"

"I know you!" responded the boy, with the readiness and boldness quite uncommon for him, "I've found Jesus! and I hope I'll stick to him."

"God bless you, my boy!" added the stranger, his large black eyes glistening with tear-drops, as they gazed into Harry's, which sparkled like wells of joy.

"Harry and I have become intimate friends," said Mr. Williams. "I have no doubt but he is a

Christian. Harry, this is Mr. Harris, the minister who is to help us in the Sunday school."

Mr. Harris was made glad by a full account of the good work at the harbor; and his heart swelled with gratitude, and he shed tears of joy, when he learned how God had blessed the influence of his former casual visit. He embraced Harry, as the first fruit of a mission already begun, and which was hence forth to be prosecuted with a quickened zeal and confirmed faith.

CHAPTER XV.

The School House.

MR. Williams was a man with common sense. He was ever consulting the fitness of things, and making that nice adjustment of matters which not only enabled him to *do* a great deal in a good undertaking, but saved him from *undoing.*

When the minister arrived, he took him, forthwith, to see Mr. Alton. This he felt to be a matter of courtesy and wisdom. Mr. Alton was a man of natural kindness and generosity, and, though not professedly religious, would be interested in any thing that tended to the general advancement of the community; and his approval and cooperation in the cause of Christ were a proper object to be sought, not to speak of the general respect he was entitled to from his important position.

Mr. Alton met the visitors with marked courtesy, and the interview was one of interest.

"You have quite an interesting community here," said Mr. Harris.

"Rather thrifty for a two-year old," responded Mr. Alton.

"Of course, you have not yet all the improvements desirable; but they will, no doubt, come to pass in due time. You must feel the need of a school, with so many children growing up without proper employment and training?"

"Very much, sir."

"What is the prospect for such advantage,—permit me to inquire?"

"Not very flattering. All the real estate of the village and country, for some miles distant, is owned by the iron company. They have no interest in the community beyond money-making. So they will not be likely to be the movers in getting up a school, nearly all the expense of which will come out their pockets. And, up to the present, the inhabitants have not had interest enough in such matters to demand their rights of those who have the entire control of real estate, or to make any special arrangement among themselves."

"Building the schoolhouse would be the main difficulty, I presume," added Mr. Williams, who had fully inquired into the matter some time before.

"The house once provided, I think a school might be gotten up," added Mr. Alton.

"Is there no building in the village, that might serve as a temporary arrangement for the present?" inquired Mr. Harris.

"Nothing but a log building, formerly used as a granary, which is now empty," answered Mr. Alton, with a smile that quite betrayed his doubtfulness as to the fitness of the building in question.

"It strikes me that might be made to answer the purpose," said Mr. Harris.

"Where there's a will there's a way," added Mr. Alton pleasantly. "It has a good roof in case of a storm, and I have a few windows on hand that might be put in."

"Rough desks might be gotten up in a few hours, and almost any thing would do for seats," rejoined Mr. Williams, who was becoming quite inspired with the idea.

"Well, indeed, I don't know but the thing might be done," concluded Mr. Alton.

"Certainly, certainly!" exclaimed Mr. Harris, who felt really happy over the new plan.

In less than two weeks, the plan had been carried into effect. The granary, thoroughly cleansed, improved by several large windows, furnished with long, old-fashioned desks along the walls, and seats of slabs, supported by large wooden pins, was really converted into a schoolhouse.

Miss Elliot was chosen teacher; and never did schoolmistress enter upon her sphere with broader and deeper views of her responsibility, and the nobleness of her calling: surely, never did a purer, lovelier spirit adorn the schoolroom. In all respects, she was fully qualified for her work.

She entered upon her duties with a full house. For the most part, she was surrounded by very crude beginnings of human life: but she knew that in each little casket there dwelt an immortal soul; and who could tell but that an angel might be hewn out of some of these rough blocks from Nature's quarry? Each character was carefully studied, and its peculiarities noted; and, after the teacher had made a full inventory of her weaknesses, she committed herself in humble trust to Him who has said,

"If any lack wisdom, let him ask of God, who giveth to all liberally and upbraideth not."

CHAPTER XVI.

The Children's Meeting.

MR. Harris had a fair knowledge of human nature, in contact with the gospel truth. He did not despair of the conversion of those advanced in life; but his largest hopes and strongest efforts were for the young; for in that period of life he had reaped most of the fruits of his ministry. In his new field of labor, no one, however aged or hardened in sin, was passed by; but he saw, that in the children of the Sunday school must be the centre of religious influence. Here was a profound and tender interest, which reached every boy and girl in the community, and which, in the hearts of some half dozen, was intensified into real Christian experience.

In addition to the Sabbath services, he wished to have some social religious exercises during the week, and determined to commence with a children's meeting. It was not publicly announced at first; but the few most prepared for the work were got together privately, and instructed as to the way of performing their part.

Very soon a meeting was given out at the schoolhouse for all the children in the place; and there was a full attendance. For the sake of those interested in such a meeting, and we trust they are not a few, we will describe it.

In many respects, it was a model meeting to some of our village and city children, who are in religious gatherings so frequently that they pay them about as little reverence as they would a tea-party. Here, the children step into the house softly, and sit in their seats as if in the presence of God. Listen! there is no whispering, no laughing, no shuffling of feet on the floor. All is still as death, except the slight rustle of the leaves as Mr. Harris finds his hymns and chapter. They sing so softly, so devoutly,—

> "Jesus loves me, this I know,
>
> For the Bible tells me so."

They all kneel down; and Mr. Harris leads in a simple, earnest prayer, in which all the children silently take part.

They rise and sing again,—

> "Oh, how happy they are whom their
>
> Savior obey,
>
> And have laid up their treasures above!"

Then Mr. Harris explained in simple language the parable of the prodigal son.

"How foolish and ungrateful was this son!" said he. "He had a beautiful home, and a kind father

156

that ought to have made any child happy; but he was not content. So reckless was he, that he asked his father for his share of the property, and, having received it, went out into the world to seek pleasure. He went into the worst company, fell into the vilest habits, and spent all he had in gratifying his lust. Then arose a famine. The crops failed, every kind of living was scarce and very expensive, and the people famished with hunger. Then this young man began to be in want. He was poor and friendless, and reduced almost to starvation. He hired himself out in the lowest business the country could afford,—that of feeding swine. He was so famished that he longed to partake of even the food which the swine ate, and no one helped him. This brought him to his senses. 'How foolish I am!' said he. 'In my father's house is bread enough and to spare, and I am perishing with hunger. I will arise and go to my father, and confess to him how wicked I have been; that I am no longer worthy to

157

be called his son; that I shall be glad to be one of his hired servants, and occupy the meanest place in the household.' His father, good old man! had been watching for him all the time of his absence, hoping that he might come back. At length, he saw him in the distance. But could it be he,—so wearied out with his hardships, so pale and ragged and cast down? Yes: the old man was fully satisfied, while his son was yet a long distance off. His heart was moved with such tender pity and such joy that *he ran to meet him.* He fell on his neck, and kissed him! The son, all broken down with sorrow, began to make his confession; but, before he got through, his father called out to the servant to bring the best clothes, to put shoes on his bare feet, and a ring on his finger, and kill the fatted calf, and be joyful; for, said he, 'my son was lost, and is found; was dead, and is alive again.'

"So we have all been ungrateful to our heavenly Father, and wandered away into sin. So we will be wretched if we do not come back. So he loves us, and will forgive us if we return to him."

Mr. Harris gave the children an opportunity to speak for Jesus. Kitty Alton was the first one to rise. A beautiful, modest flush crept over her cheeks, and a tear glistened in her eye, as she said,—

"Jesus must be my best friend, for he has died for me. Oh, how I love him! He is so kind, he does not ask us to suffer for our sins: he suffered himself, to get salvation for us, and now only asks us to take it."

Clara Williams followed:—

"For a long time I have been trying to be good, to be a Christian," said she; "but my heart was so wicked that I failed every day. At last I have found out the true way,—we must give ourselves wholly up to Jesus, and trust in nothing but his blood for salvation. Now I have peace: now I am happy."

"I love Jesus," said Harry, so full of emotion

that he could barely speak plainly. "The boys laugh at me, but I'll never give up."

Here his heart overflowed; and he sat down, and buried his face, and wept.

In Frank Williams there was evidently a conflict. His face glowed with excitement; he moved about uneasily on his seat, and seemed several times to be making an effort to rise.

Mr. Harris's eye was on him. He understood the boy's trouble.

"Don't be afraid, Frank," said he. "Stand up for Jesus. He will help you."

Frank made a desperate effort, and rose to his feet.

"For a long time I have felt bad," said he, "because I'm such a sinner; but something has held me back from giving myself to Jesus. Now I have made up my mind to be a Christian anyhow."

"Come to Jesus," said Mr. Harris. "None but Jesus can do helpless sinners good."

He inquired if any one wished to be prayed for.

Joe Rowly, one of the largest and roughest boys in the village, sat near the door, on the end of one of the long benches. During the meeting, he had been an object of general observation, partly because of his conspicuous position, more particularly on account of the contrast between his present seriousness and his former life.

"Pray for me," said he; and, dropping his head, he covered his face with his hands, while the large tears trickled through his fingers.

All knelt down for a few minutes of silent prayer. Nothing could be heard but the suppressed sobs of several of the children. Before rising, Mr. Harris offered a brief, audible prayer, full of tenderness and devotion; and, after singing a hymn, the meeting dispersed.

As Mr. Harris was fairly in the street surrounded by his little flock, he met Andy and Toodie. They were perched on the high seat of a large two-horse wagon, a calf in behind, and a cow follow-ing,—all of which was property of their highly esteemed employer, Mr. Alton. As usual, they were overflowing with good-nature; and their large, coarse, ebony faces, all aglow with Christian kindliness, seemed really beautiful.

"Dat's de plan, Broder Harris. Begin at de beginnin'," said Andy. "More hope for de young den for old sinners. It's easy 'nough to bend de slender saplin'; but when de tree gits old and stout, an' all de juice is dried up, its mighty tough takin' de crooks out."

"True enough," added Mr. Harris. "Besides, these little fellows are the doorkeepers of the par-ents' hearts."

"Dat's so. Jest look here, Broder Harris," con-tinued Andy, as he pointed at the cow stretching her neck to the utmost to touch the calf with her tongue, and muttering with satisfaction as she lav-ished upon it her rude caresses. "Squire Alton sent me over to Garden Bay, some six miles from here, to bring home this ar' cow an' calf, which he'd jest bought of George Thomson. Thomson was puzzled to know how I'd git de cow home. I sez, 'Neber you mind. Put de calf in de wagon, an' I'll risk de cow.' You see she's jist follered close on to de wagon, ebery step of de way."

"Take de lambs in your arms, an' de sheep 'ill foller," added Toodie. "Did you have a good meetin'?"

"Very good. The Lord is at work in those young hearts," answered Mr. Harris as he pointed emphatically towards the little company moving on into the village.

"Bress de Lord! Den de ole folks 'ill soon be comin'," Andy prophesied, as he snapped his whip, and went on.

CHAPTER XVII.

Plants, and what they teach.

R. Harris recognized the great fact, that the Holy Spirit influences men through the natural laws of their being. This was a great help to him in his ministry; for it led him to study human nature, and to use the laws of mind and the relations of life as channels for reaching the human heart.

He saw that the social power was a great means of good; that by coming in contact with man's daily life, and obtaining a place in his affections, a strong vantage-ground was gained for bringing him to a knowledge of the truth; so he gave his attention to it with a sense of responsibility. He frequently had social gatherings at his house, sometimes of the old, and sometimes of the young; they were always made the occasion of spiritual profit.

In this arrangement, his wife, who was a quiet, earnest spirit, took as much interest as himself. She would make the most ample preparations for such an occasion, and throw open every room in the house, that every visitor might feel perfectly at home.

As Mr. and Mrs. Harris were intensely fond of children, and regarded them as the most promising subjects of Christian effort, the invitation was most frequently given out for them.

On one such occasion, when nearly all the little ones in the village were gathered at the minister's pleasant home, he gave them a most interesting talk about plants and flowers. The idea was readily suggested, for the pastor's sitting-room was a small greenhouse.

"Those geraniums, and that Chinese primrose, I have had ever since I was a student in the theological seminary," said Mr. Harris, pointing out several most beautiful specimens of plant-life, as the little company gazed with wonder on the great variety of plants and flowers, which nearly filled up the two large front windows; "and I remember some interesting facts about them."

Mr. Harris saw that all were anxious to hear what he had to say; so he went on.

"I then had my first experience in taking care of plants. A friend made me a present of a few; and I went to the greenhouse, and bought more, till my window, which was on the sunny side of the building, was nearly filled up. I watered them regularly, and watched them with a tender interest; and every one said they were doing well. After I had had them several weeks, I perceived that both the leaves and the flowers seemed to be turning toward the window. I turned around a large scarlet geranium which stood in a prominent place, and oh, the profusion of bright, rich leaves, the clusters of buds and blossoms! It seemed almost wholly one-sided. I turned round all the rest, and was astonished and delighted with the changed appearance of my window. Every plant teemed with foliage and blossoms.

"In a few days, however, the whole scene had changed. Every leaf, bud, and blossom had turned to the window again. They would seek the sunshine; and, if I would preserve their symmetry and beauty, I must keep constantly turning them, and thus give every part the benefit of light and warmth.

"By and by I was sick for several weeks; and a fellow-student, who roomed in the opposite side of the building, and whose window was never cheered with a ray of sunshine, took my plants to his apartment, to care for them during my illness. He watered them regularly, and did his best to keep them thrifty; but gradually the blossoms faded and dropped off, the leaves withered, and the tender shoots lost their vitality.

"My friend became alarmed for them, and brought them to my room with much anxiety, declaring that he had done his utmost to make them flourish. The plants were returned to my window, and gradually recovered their thrift and beauty."

"I've seen turnip-tops and potato-stalks grow in the cellar," said Harry; "but they're very pale."

"Certainly," said Mr. Harris, "and very feeble. They never could have come to any thing without light. All plants and vegetables must have light."

"Just as all Christians must live in the light of Christ," said Clara Williams to Kitty Alton.

"You are right, Clara," said Mr. Harris, who had been waiting to see if anyone would draw the moral. "Christ is called *'Light,'* and in him is no darkness. No Christian can be either happy or useful, except as he dwells in that Light.

"To return to my story: my fellow-students were highly pleased with my plants; and very soon, by means of friends and the greenhouse, many of them had ornamented their windows in a similar manner. Mr. S., my next-door neighbor, had quite a selection of geraniums, roses, primroses, pinks, &c., and also a very fine hanging-basket, containing a great variety of the most delicate vines, the gift of a particular friend.

"I had been to his room several times to see his treasures, and he seemed much pleased with my admiration of them.

"One day, he brought his hanging-basket to my room, looking exceedingly serious.

"'What do you think ails these vines?' said he, in a sad tone, as he held them up, wilted and faded, and having lost half their leaves.

"'Have you taken good care of them?' I inquired.

"'Certainly,' said he. 'I have watered them once a week regularly, have turned all the pots around every now and then, and picked off all the dead leaves; and yet see how these vines are dying, and every plant in my window is fading and drying up.'

"'The case is very clear,' said I. 'They need more water. They should be watered every day regularly. And the hanging-basket, which is especially exposed to the dry air and high temperature of the room, as it is of open work, should be put in a large dish of water and thoroughly saturated. Plants must have their full amount of water regularly, or they cannot flourish.'"

"Just as we must read the Bible, and pray every day, and go to the prayer-meetin's and the preachin', or our souls can't git along well," said Harry.

"You have applied the matter correctly," replied Mr. Harris. "Prayer, the Word of God, and the sanctuary, are God's appointed means of grace; and the Christian needs them regularly, just as truly as plants need water."

Mr. Harris's talk about plants was highly interesting and profitable to the children, as much so as any sermon they had ever heard.

But Mr. Harris knew that the mind needs amusement as well as devotion. So, picture-books, music, and various other innocent diversions, were summoned to the occasion. And, when the day was spent, the children returned home, hoping that the time might not be long till they should have another visit at the pleasant home of their pastor.

CHAPTER XVIII.

The Church Formed.

IN the physical world, God promotes life by organism. Vegetable life expands in the form of a stalk or a tree, which blossoms, and brings forth fruit; and one stalk or tree begets others. So, in the moral world, men have learned that life and power are secured by organized societies. The Christians at the harbor recognized this fact, and formed themselves into a church.

A Sabbath Day was set apart for the services of the occasion; and, as it was something altogether new, and a deep religious interest was spreading in the community, nearly all the town was present. The appointment was made at the schoolhouse; but very soon it was so crowded that an out-door meeting was proposed.

The congregation adjourned to a beautiful little nook by the lake, on the side of the point opposite the harbor. It was nearly semi-circular, and shaded by a thicket of cedars. Here, as by the Sea of Galilee when Christ was on earth, the people stood on the shore, and listened to the Word of God.

All nature seemed to smile on the occasion. Not a cloud was in the sky. The air was balmy, and so clear that distant objects lost their perspective. Indian Bluff, in its garment of evergreens, and islands many miles from the point, seemed to come so near that one might almost fancy them within the audience.

There was a tender melody in the singing, as it swelled out upon the water, and rang among the hills; prayer seemed unusually fervent, and the dis-

"The congregation adjourned to a beautiful little nook by the lake."—Page 173.

course was practical and earnest. But more impressive than anything else was the public acknowledgment of Christ by four of the Sunday-school children. Clara and Frank Williams, Kitty Alton and Harry, came out from among the world, and put on Christ in baptism. Their tenderness in years, and deep sincerity, touched every heart; and many tears were shed while they received the sacred ordinance, "in the name of the Father, and of the Son, and of the Holy Ghost." It was a sight truly beautiful.

Morning service ended, and another was held, near the close of the day, at the same place. The evening was no less beautiful than the morning. There was a soft violet haze in the atmosphere, that enriched the landscape; and gorgeous clouds which gathered about the setting sun cast a crimson light upon the lake. What in nature is more impressive than the close of a beautiful day! There is something in its fading loveliness and shadowy solemnity that quiets the turbulent passions of the soul, and calls up all that is sacred and tender in our nature. It had its effect on the humble little audience by the lake, as they sang the song of praise, offered prayer, and listened to the Word. Nor is it strange that nature, in its numberless phases of beauty, should aid us in receiving the written revelation: the Author of the Bible is also the Author of the world, and can speak to us through them both.

An impressive sermon had been preached from the words, "I must work the work of Him that sent me, while it is day: the night cometh, when no man can work." The day had faded into twilight, and the service was about to close. The last exercise was the formal constituting of the church. Those who were to be members stood on the shore, facing the audience. There were fourteen,—ten adults, and the four children who had that day put on Christ in public profession. The men and women stood in a row, with the four little ones in front, while they took upon them the solemn vows of church-obligation.

The doxology swelled forth with that peculiar pathos which is born of deep emotion; and the congregation dispersed, never to forget the scenes of that day.

CHAPTER XIX.

Mr. Alton's Conviction.

OW shall we increase the attendance at the prayer-meeting?" said Mr. Williams one day, at the close of the weekly gathering of adults for that purpose.

This prayer-meeting for the older portion of the community had recently been established, in addition to that for the children referred to before; and, beyond the few professors of religion, it was difficult to secure attendance.

The above question was put to the congregation just before dispersing; and Mr. Harris immediately presented a plan in reply:—

"Let us turn ourselves into a recruiting company, and, as we go out from here, invite the first person we meet to meet with us next Wednesday afternoon, at three o'clock; then continue our invitation wherever we go."

The plan commended itself, and all adopted it. Kittie Alton, as all the rest of the little Christians, was present, and started home on the alert to carry it out.

The first person she met was her father.

"Papa, will you go to prayer-meeting with me next Wednesday afternoon, at three o'clock? Mr. Harris wants everybody to come," she said, before fairly up to him.

"Kittie, I don't want you to speak to me about that again. Now remember," replied her father, as he stood before her, and looked her sternly in the face for a moment, and then walked on.

Kittie passed him, and went home almost heartbroken. What could make her father answer her so? He never had done so before. The stern answer, uttered in such harsh tones, had wounded her very heart; and she walked on in company with Clara Williams, scarcely able to speak.

Her mother saw the sad cloud on her brow as she entered the door, and wondered what could have darkened the joy that had so filled her heart ever since the experience of her new life in Christ. But Mrs. Alton was a stranger to that life, and stood aloof from it as something mysterious and awful, into which she dared not inquire.

Kittie felt the need of Christian sympathy at home every hour; but she had learned to carry her burdens to her Savior. With scarcely a word, she passed on to her room; and, laying by her hat and shawl, kneeled down by her little bed and prayed,—

"Oh, God! Teach my father how to be a Christian. Show him his need of thee, and give him a new heart. Oh that he may go to the prayer-meeting with me, and help me in the good way!"

There was a long pause, and heavy sobs, and then another petition:—

"O God, have mercy on my mother! Make her a Christian."

For a few moments, she remained on her knees, bowed over on her face, and then rose with the peace of God in her heart.

Mr. Alton had gone to his office, anxious to employ every moment, for his business was pressing. But, somehow, he felt very uneasy, and made slow progress at his desk. In his confusion, he pulled open the wrong drawer, opened the wrong file of papers; and, when he took up his pen, he thought one thing and wrote another. He felt troubled in the way he had answered Kittie. Her kind little face, so full of sadness at his harsh reply, came between him and every object he tried to see. Why did he speak to her so? He queried, but could not answer.

Mr. Alton was, without doubt, a kind-hearted man, and scarcely ever uttered an unkind word. His ordinary temptations did not lie in that direction. But now his whole being was thrown into commotion, and the evil passions of his carnal heart were showing themselves without disguise.

He was under conviction of sin. The new religious influence in the place, in Kittie's new life, were having a great effect upon him. He could no longer trust in his morality: he was becoming conscious that there was a depth of depravity in his heart that he could not fathom. The Christian religion was evidently the one thing needful; and he had never experienced it.

Satan does not give up the human heart without a dreadful struggle. As in the case of the child in the Gospels, he casts us down, and throws us into the most painful convulsions before he leaves us. Just before conversion, we frequently find the most amiable disposition unamiable, and those who are naturally patient and forbearing, exceedingly fretful and unkind. But, if the terrible conflict ends in yielding the will to God, a sweet peace follows, and the individual sits at the feet of Jesus, clothed and in his right mind.

Mr. Alton opened his ledger, and ran down the long column of names of debtors to the iron company. A voice seemed to speak to his heart, as in tones of thunder, "You have an account to settle with your God. How does it stand?" His past life came up before him. Oh, the neglected offers of mercy! the duties left undone! the sins in word and thought and deed! He trembled as he thought of the day when the dead, small and great, shall stand before God, and the book shall be opened; and the dead shall be judged out of the things written in the books according to their works. But he summoned every energy to silence his convictions, and drown his thoughts in the business of the hour.

Happy for men, that God does not always give them the desire of their hearts; that the Holy Spirit continues long in its tender pleadings.

CHAPTER XX.

A Joyful Event.

"MA won't you pray with me?" said Kittie to her mother the evening following, as her mother was about to put her to bed.

Never had Mrs. Alton met so perplexing a question. For a moment she was speechless, as Kittie's beautiful eyes were fixed upon her, and her arms entwined imploringly about her neck.

"I cannot pray, Kittie," said she at length. "I do not know how."

"If you try, Ma, God will teach you how."

Mrs. Alton kissed her little girl in reply, and

kneeled by her side, as she uttered her simple, child-like petition to her Father in heaven.

"Haven't you noticed a great change in our little girl since she has become a Christian?" said Mrs. Alton to her husband, as she returned to the sitting-room, where he was busy over his weekly newspaper.

"I have noticed a very great change," said he, his eyes still fixed on his paper.

"What do you think of it?" continued Mrs. Alton seriously. "You know you and I have never had much faith in religion."

"It puzzles me," answered Mr. Alton, as he laid by his paper. "I am afraid we have not done our duty by the child. We have been a hindrance to her when we should have been a help."

Mr. Alton especially had reason for reflection. He had opposed Kittie seriously at the time she united with the church, giving his consent only after the child's most earnest entreaty. Then, he well knew that his constant indifference towards the struggles of her new life must be very disheartening, not to speak of his unkind answer to her in the afternoon.

"Don't you think it is time for us to lead a new life?" inquired Mrs. Alton, after a pause. "It would be a terrible thing to lay stumbling blocks in our child's way."

"You are right. God only knows our responsibility. We dare not treat it lightly. This has troubled me for the last few days more than I can tell."

"I fear that we have been too easily satisfied in our doubts as to Christianity. It is an awful question, and should have the most careful and serious attention."

"I must confess, where I thought I saw objections without number, there now appears to be none. Evidently the difficulty has been in our hearts."

A long and serious conversation followed, and

the husband and wife discovered in each other the deepest religious conviction. They could not retire that night without prayer; but who was to pray? Each asked the other to do so, but both refused. All their life they had neglected that duty, and now it seemed impossible to begin.

If the unconverted would know how estranged they are from God let them try to pray.

"I do not know who can pray for us tonight, unless it be Kittie," said Mrs. Alton.

The little girl was called up at midnight, to pray with her father and mother. Kneeling down between them, in her snowy night-robe, and folding her hands devoutly, she prayed out of a full heart. With many tears Mr. and Mrs. Alton followed, and, making a full consecration rose conscious of the new life in Christ.

It was a glorious night to the little family and, no doubt, angels in heaven rejoiced with Kittie, as she embraced now her father and now her mother, mingling her tears of joy with theirs over their new-found hope.

CHAPTER XXI.

Objections Met.

THE conversion of Mr. and Mrs. Alton made a great sensation in the community. Mr. Alton's position was such, that the very fact of his becoming religious was influential; and the change in his life was so great, as to be remarked by everyone.

Dr. Sprague especially was moved by this unlooked-for event. Seldom is the life of two men more closely connected, than his and Mr. Alton's had been, since their acquaintance at the harbor.

They were the chief managers of the business of the company, were similar in their sentiments, tastes, and habits, for the most part had been cut off from intercourse with their own class in society, and had become very strongly attached to each other. When Mr. Alton became a new man in heart and life, and seemed to enter into a new world, the doctor felt as if he were left alone.

He seldom spoke of matters of religion. Scarcely any one knew his sentiments of the subject. But, as far as his thoughts had gone, he was decidedly skeptical. He acknowledged the change in Mr. Alton, however, and was anxious to have a confidential talk with him, but hesitated to make the beginning. Mr. Alton was quite as anxious to talk with him, but, somehow, could open his heart more easily to almost any one else.

Several days passed before the subject was broken between them. But the matter had grown into a sense of responsibility with Mr. Alton, and he determined to do his duty.

"Take a seat, doctor. I want to have a private talk with you," said he one morning, as the doctor came into his office.

"At your service, sir," replied the doctor with his usual air of pleasantry, as he took the easy-chair in the corner, while Mr. Alton closed the door.

"I am exceedingly anxious for you to become a Christian," said the latter, as he took his seat directly in front of his friend.

"My mind is full of doubts and objections on the subject of Christianity," answered the doctor calmly, but with decision.

"Just as mine used to be. And, be assured, no one can ever remove them for you. Somehow, mere arguments, however logical, fail to bring the mind to a conclusion. When you are overwhelmed by them, you may seem to bury your doubts; but in the hour of calm reflection they will rise again. Moral and religious questions are too much for the mere intellect to settle. Personal experience alone is conclusive."

"Do you mean that all argument, even for the purpose of honest inquiry is useless?"

"In a certain sense, it is not. The truths of Christianity have nothing to lose by discussion. There are evidences which none can deny. But the difficulty, in unbelief, lies far below the reach of mere reason. It is in the *affections,* in the *will,* in the *heart.* So long as that is held in reserve, all is darkness. But, if any one will do the will of God, he shall know concerning the doctrine."

"That doesn't do much for a man's stumbling-blocks," rejoined the doctor with a smile.

"Very true. And you can put to me a hundred objections against Christianity, which I cannot answer; yet there is within me a consciousness of its reality, which it is impossible to disturb. I know the truth of religion as I know my life. It is a matter of experience."

Somehow the doctor felt uneasy under the conversation, and rose to leave.

"Think of this matter, doctor," urged Mr. Alton. "You cannot afford to pass it by."

The doctor went to his home much dissatisfied with the position taken by Mr. Alton. Why should he thus shut off all his skeptical inquiries? Was it not the part of Christian duty to solve them?

No sooner had he entered the house when he broached the subject to Miss Elliott.

"In some respects," said he, "it seems to me Alton's religion has not done much for him."

"How is that?" replied Miss Elliott.

"He refuses attention to a single difficulty in religious doctrine."

"That is not strange. When first converted, one cares but little for argument. Every thing is *life*. Besides, argument can do but little for those who have no experience. But what are your questions?"

"Why is there so much hypocrisy among professors of religion?"

"Why is there so much counterfeit money?" added Miss Elliott.

The doctor was silent.

"Because of the value of genuine money," replied Miss Elliott, in answer to her own question. "Who cares to counterfeit that which is of no value? Viewed from the right standpoint, hypocrisy is itself an argument for the truth of religion. But it is quite possible to exaggerate the faults of professors of Christianity."

"I can find those outside the church that are better than many who are in it," rejoined the doctor.

"Certainly. It would be strange if it were not so. But how do you make your comparison? You take the best man you can find out of the church, and compare him with the worst one you can find in it. Is that fair? Besides, what would your best man out of the church have been, had it not been for the influence of that high moral sentiment which the world has received through the church? Then, perhaps, you begin your investigation of character with a slight prejudice which works like a spyglass. You look through it one way, and the virtues of the man of the world are magnified: you turn it around, and those of the Christian professor are diminished."

"Why are there so many religious sects?" continued the doctor.

"There are no more sects in religion than there are in the sciences; and it may be doubted that the disputes of theologians have ever been as sharp as those of philosophers. Even the profession of medicine has about as many sects as the church. Nothing is more common among men than difference of opinion."

"Is it easy for you to believe in the miracles of the Bible?"

"Is it easy for you to believe there is a God?"

"I cannot doubt the existence of a God," replied

the doctor. "To my mind, this world must have a cause; and it is so full of means to ends, of intelligent design, that I am compelled to believe in a personal First Cause. More over, my conscience teaches me, that I am constituted under law, under a Supreme Lawgiver. I should think a man either simple or obstinate who did not believe in a God."

"Does it seem reasonable, that that God, in whom you are compelled to believe, should reveal himself to his creatures?—should communicate with his children?"

"Certainly."

"How could he have done it without miracles?"

A puzzled smile was the only reply the doctor could make.

"A messenger from God to men must need perform miracles," continued Miss Elliott, "not to prove his doctrine, but to prove his authority as a teacher,—to commend himself to the world as Christ commended himself to the common sense of

Nicodemus, when that ruler said, 'We know that thou art a teacher come from God; for no man can do these miracles that thou doest, except God be with him.'"

"Is not a miracle contrary to nature?"

"I do not see that it is. It is something *more* than nature,—something *added to it,* but not necessarily contrary to it. And, if you believe in a God of unlimited power, miracles are not unreasonable. He who is the author of the great system of nature should be able to lay his hand upon it, and control it at his will,—should be able to manifest power above and beyond its laws, just as a watchmaker should be able to interfere with his watch, and move it forward and backward as he saw fit."

"What about the contradictions of the Bible?"

"Are you sure there are any?"

"Certainly. I met a man at Escanaba, the other day, who had a small pamphlet full of them."

"Indeed! Can you remember any of them?"

"In the sixth chapter of Galatians is a contradiction, with only two verses between. One passage says, "Bear ye one another's burdens, and so fulfil the law of Christ:' the other says, 'Every man shall bear his own burden.'"

"Those passages may both be true, without the least contradiction. A careful reading will show that *'Burden'* has a different meaning in the two passages. In the first it signifies *fault* or *weakness*. *Bear with one another's faults, or weaknesses.* In the second, it means *accountability. Every one must bear his own accountability.* I don't see much contradiction there. Is there any other?"

"Yes. In one place the command is, *'Honor* thy father and thy mother;' in another, 'Husbands *love* your wives, and *be not bitter against them.'* And yet Jesus Christ says, 'If any man come to me, and *hate* not his father and mother, and wife and children, and brethren and sisters, yea, and his own life also, he cannot be my disciple.'"

"Here is not a *contradiction*, but a *comparison*,—a comparison expressed in hyperbolic language, common enough anywhere, but especially familiar to the Orientals. Our Savior's discourses are full of it. No one loves his father, mother, wife, children, &c., as truly as does the Christian. His religious experience elevates and purifies all the sanctities of life; but his love for Christ is so much greater than all other affections, that, compared with it, they are as mere hatred. The last part of Christ explains the rest. No sane person ever hated his own life. The martyrs loved their lives in the best sense; but so supreme was their love for Christ, that it was as if they hated their own life."

"What about the manner of Christ's death?" continued the doctor, fully routed from every position he had taken. "Do you think he really sweat blood?"

"That is an interesting question to you, as a

physician; and the investigation of it has thrown much light on the New Testament. Luke is the only evangelist who gives an account of Christ's bloody sweat in the Garden of Gethsemane. He was a physician; and, on examination, it is found that the account is given in the most scientific terms. Dr. Stroud, a celebrated English physician, has written a thorough work on the death of Christ, in which he takes a special note of its physiological facts. It is a learned production, and fully justifies the sacred narrative. Through a friend of mine, I have procured notes from it, which I think I can find in a few minutes; and I shall be glad to read them to you."

"Please do so," said the doctor: "that is a very interesting subject."

Miss Elliott soon found the notes, and read as follows: [1]"One of the principle corporeal effects of the exciting passions is palpitation, or vehement

[1] Dr. Stroud's *Death of Christ*, pp. 85, 86, 87, 88.

action, of the heart; and it will now be shown, that, when this action is intense it produces bloody sweat, dilatation, and ultimately rupture of the heart. By those acquainted with the structure and functions of the animal frame, such results might readily be anticipated. Perspiration, both sensible and insensible, takes place from the mouths or small regularly organized tubes, which perforate the skin in all parts of the body, terminating in blind extremities internally, and by innumerable orifices on the outer surface. These tubes are surrounded by a network of minute vessels, and penetrated by the ultimate ramifications of arteries which, according to the force of the local circulation, depend chiefly on that of the heart, discharge either the watery parts of the blood in the state of vapor, its grosser ingredients in the form of a glutinous liquid, or, in extreme cases, the entire blood itself. The influence of the invigorating passions, more especially an exciting and increased flow of blood to the skin, is familiarly illustrated by the process of blushing, either from shame or anger; for during this state the heart beats strongly, the surface of the body becomes hot and red, and, if the emotion is very powerful, breaks out into a warm and copious perspiration,—the first step towards a bloody sweat.'"

"That theory is very good as far as the bloody sweat is concerned," said the doctor. "The points are well taken as to the relation of the small blood-vessels to the pores of the body, through which perspiration takes place. But what about the historical facts of the case? Has an incident of bloody sweat ever been found?"

Miss Elliott read, "'The eminent French historian, De Thou, mentions the case of "an Italian officer who commanded at Monte-Maro, a fortress of Piedmont, during the war of 1522, between Henry II. of France and the Emperor, Charles V. This officer having been treacherously seized by order of the hostile general, and threatened with public execution unless he surrendered the place, was so agitated at the prospect of an ignominious death that he sweated blood from every part of his body.' The same writer relates a similar occurrence in the person of a young Florentine at Rome, unjustly put to death by order of Pope Sixtus V., in the beginning of his reign; and concludes the narrative as follows:

"'When the youth was led forth to execution, he excited the commiseration of many; and, through excess of grief, was observed to shed bloody tears, and to discharge blood instead of sweat from his whole body,—a circumstance which many regarded as a certain proof that nature condemned the severity of a sentence so cruelly hastened, and invoked vengeance against the magistrate himself, as therein guilty of the murder.' Amongst several examples given in "The German Ephemerides," of bloody tears and bloody sweat occasioned by extreme fear, more especially the fear of death, may be mentioned that of "a young boy, who having taken part in a crime for which two of his elder brothers were hanged, was exposed to public view under the gallows on which they were executed, and was thereupon observed to sweat blood from his whole body."

"'In his commentaries on the four Gospels, Maldonato refers to "a robust and healthy man at Paris, who on hearing sentence of death passed on him, was covered with a bloody sweat." Schench sites from a martyrology the case of "a nun who fell into the hands of soldiers; and, on seeing herself compassed with swords and daggers, threatening instant death, was so terrified and agitated that she discharged blood from every part of her body, and died of hæmorrhage in the sight of her assailants." And Tissot reports from a respectable journal that of "a sailor who was so alarmed by a storm, that, through fear, he fell down; and his face sweated blood, which, during the whole continuance of the storm, returned like ordinary sweat as fast as it was wiped away.""""

"That is exceedingly interesting, and quite satisfactory," said the doctor. "What does your author say to the blood and water which came from the side of Christ when the soldier pierced him, just before he was taken down from the cross?"

"He first gives the physiological theory of the phenomena, and then cites well authenticated cases of death by rupture of the heart, which are shown to be illustrative of Christ's death."

"That is exactly to the point. Let us hear it."

Miss Elliott read again, [2]"The actions of the heart, which are maintained during the whole of life with admirable energy and regularity, are liable to be deranged by various causes, and particularly by the passions of the mind. It is observed by Baron Haller, the father of modern physiology, that "excessive grief occasions palpitation, and some-

---

[2] Dr. Stroud's *Death of Christ*, page 76.

206

times sudden death; that the corporeal effects of anger and terror are nearly alike, including increased strength and violent motions, both in the heart and throughout the body, and producing bloody sweats and other kinds of hæmorrhage . . . Fear and terror are powerful causes, especially when they seize suddenly. In that case, the nerves act with violence on the heart, and derange the order of its movements. The blood is at the same time propelled in these passions by a general shock, or commotion of all the parts of the body: and therefore it necessarily accumulates in the two trunks of the *venæ curvæ* (the large veins which return the blood to the heart), rushes into the auricles (the upper chambers of the heart).'[3] . . . 'The immediate cause (of rupture of the heart) is a sudden and violent contraction of one of the ventricles, usually the left, on the column of blood thrown into

---

[3] Page 88.

it by a similar contraction of the corresponding auricle.[4]   Prevented from returning backwards by the intervening valve, and not finding a sufficient outlet forwards in the connected artery, the blood re-acts against the ventricle itself, which is consequently torn open at the point of greatest distension, or least resistance, by its own reflected force. A quantity of blood is hereby discharged into the pericardium;[5] and, having no means of escape from that capsule, stops the circulation by compressing the heart from without, and induces almost instantaneous death. In young and vigorous subjects, the blood thus collected in the pericardium soon divides itself into its constituent parts, namely, a pale, watery liquid called serum, and a soft, clotted substance of a deep red color, termed crassamentum.'

"So much for the general explanation of the fact

---

[4] Page 77.

[5] A sack in which the heart is enclosed.

of the rupture of the heart," said Miss Elliott. "I will now give you the cases sighted from good authorities.

[6]"Dr. Fischer, a German, furnishes the following: 'A gentleman, aged sixty-eight, and apparently possessing every claim to long life, after having spent many years at court, was compelled to quit it, and retired to a country residence . . . Towards the close of life, his attention was occupied by an unpleasant business, which, interfering with the indulgence of his propensity for solitude, had the effect of aggravating his melancholy. On the 16th of October, 1817, he was seized, whilst walking, with a severe pain, which he supposed to be a cramp at the stomach. This pain, after returning repeatedly, attended with violent agitation and agony, proved fatal on the evening of the twentieth. On examination of the body after death, the only morbid condition of any importance was rupture of

----

[6] Page 97.

the heart.'

"Mr. Townsend of New York says, 'An unfortunate female of this city literally and truly died of a broken heart, as was found on dissection; and there was every reason to believe that this consummation of her misery was the unavoidable consequence of her exquisite dejection of mind at that particular moment. She was twenty-two years of age, robust, and long addicted to dissolute and intemperate habits. For some time previous to her decease, she had complained only of slight, and apparently rheumatic pains; but, within a day or two of the fatal event, she had been deserted by a man to whom she was engaged in marriage. In consequence of this, her mind became very deeply affected. After having supped on the preceding night, she retired to rest as usual, and in the morning was found dead in bed. On dissection, the sack of the pericardium was found filled with about ten ounces of coagulated blood, and two of serum. The breech in the heart was irregular and lacerated, and about half an inch in diameter.' Doctor Williams of Southampton gives the following account: 'R.W., a laborer, aged fifty-six years, had generally enjoyed good health; but for ten years had suffered great despondency of mind, owing to domestic trouble. About six months before his death, he was troubled with a severe cough, which came on in paroxysms, generally at night and early in the morning; and, after a fit of this kind, was found one morning dead. A postmortem examination took place in the presence of Mr. Boulton, surgeon, of Leamington. On opening the chest, the bag of the pericardium appeared much distended with fluid, and was of a dark blue color. On cutting into it, a pint, at least, of transparent serum issued out, leaving the crassamentum firmly attached to the anterior surface of the heart. On further examination, the heart was found to be ruptured.' The following case, related by Mr. Adams, is remarkably similar: 'Thomas

Treacher, forty-six years of age, a stout, muscular working-man, who had labored many years under great mental anxiety, was attacked with severe cardiac symptoms on Sunday evening, November the 5th, 1826; and, after great agony of body and mind, died on November the 9th. The pericardium was found distended, and, when divided, emitted a quantity of serous fluid; but the heart was entirely concealed by an envelope of coagulated blood in three distinct layers, owing to rupture of the left ventricle.'"

"That is intensely interesting," said the doctor, as Miss Elliott laid her manuscript on the table. "Where did you get those notes?"

"A friend of mine copied them from Dr. Stroud's work on the death of Christ, which is in the library of the late and celebrated Dr. Neander. The library is now in the Theological Seminary of Rochester, N.Y. It was there my friend took these notes. Dr. Stroud's work is one of great authority, but is now out of print. My notes are a mere selection from it. It contains well-authenticated cases of bloody sweat, and death by rupture of the heart, among the Greeks, Latins, Germans, French, and in Scotland, England, and America. In all, they would make a fair-sized volume."

"I just now recall," said the doctor, "that, during my course of lectures at the medical college, this matter was referred to by the professors; but somehow I never thought of it in connection with the death of Christ. It would seem, that, in that case, science confirms the New-Testament narrative."

"Certainly; and there are many other cases in which modern science is confirming the statements of the Word of God. It is certainly instructive to compare the facts just read with the Gospel narrative of the death of Christ. His life was one of sadness: for he bore our griefs, and carried our sorrows; and there was laid on him the iniquity of us all. During his last night on earth, while in the

213

Garden of Gethsemane, his life-long suffering was approaching its climax. He began to be sorrowful and very heavy; and exclaimed to his disciples, 'My soul is exceeding sorrowful to death.' Now he came into full consciousness of the wretched condition of our fallen human nature, of the devil and demerit of sin, of the infinite opposition of the divine holiness and justice to it, and of the necessary wrath of God against it. Then he fell with his face upon the earth; and his sweat was as it were great drops of blood, falling down to the ground, his agony being so great that he prayed the Father, if possible, to let the cup pass from him. It would seem that here his life would have ended, had there not appeared an angel from heaven, strengthening him. On the cross, his anguish was renewed, and reached its dreadful crisis. He cried out with a loud voice, 'My God, my God! why hast thou forsaken me?' He was left alone to bear up under his burden of unmitigated woe. This was too terrible for nature to support; it literally broke his heart."

"You think he died from mental anguish, rather than from bodily wounds?" said the doctor.

"It is difficult to understand why he should have died so soon, if his death had been merely from bodily exhaustion. He seems to have died before the thieves who were crucified with him; and Pilot wondered at the early announcement of his death. It would also be difficult to account for the blood and water which issued from his side, when the soldier pierced him, if he did not die of rupture of the heart."

The conversation ended. All was quiet for a few moments; Miss Elliott having resumed her sewing, and the doctor being absorbed in thought. Presently he rose and went out, confused by the clearness of Miss Elliott's reasoning against his objections to Christianity; his intellect having been carried by the force of logic, but his heart all unyielding.

Miss Elliott's thoughts went up to God for him in prayer; and she felt a fresh consciousness of hope, that the desire of her heart was not in vain.

CHAPTER XXII.

Doctor Sprague's Conversion.

N the following evening was the beginning of a series of daily meetings, held by the Christians at the harbor. The attendance was large; and Dr. Sprague had left an unusual press of business, in order to be present. He had a peculiar interest in every part of the exercise, but more especially in the words of an aged and familiar personage, who rose to speak near the close of the meeting, in a farther corner of the room. In that tall and noble figure, bent over with years, those flowing locks and beard of snowy whiteness, and that voice, tremulous with age and emotion, he recognized an old and venerable acquaintance. Father Wilson, a citizen of his former place of residence, and father-in-law of Mr. Alton, having heard the good news of the conversion of his daughter and her husband had come to rejoice with them.

There was something commanding in his personal appearance; and so touching were his words, that the audience listened with almost breathless attention. He thanked God for what had been done at the harbor, gave a personal testimony of the truth of the Christian religion from his own life, and, with large tears rolling down his cheeks, put his question to the unconverted of the congregation, "Where will you spend your eternity?"

"Can you doubt the reality of Father Wilson's Christian experience?" Miss Elliott inquired of the doctor, as soon as they had returned home. "Do you think it is possible for him to be deluded as to the truth of religion?"

"The old gentleman seems very sincere; and he has lived a noble life," replied the doctor.

"Of him, it may truly be said in the judgement, 'I was an hungred, and ye gave me meat, I was thirsty, and ye gave me drink; I was a stranger, and ye took me in; naked, and ye clothed me; I was sick, and ye visited me; I was in prison, and ye came unto me.' He has cared for many of the least of Christ's little ones, and has lavished his kindnesses on the needy of all classes. While he was speaking, I could but wonder how you would reply to him."

"With argument, one can meet argument; with sophistry, one can meet sophistry: but when a man speaks from such a heart and such a life, who that has no heart nor life to correspond shall be able to answer?"

This much the doctor's natural candor compelled him so say. In vain might he search among men of the world for an equal to Father Wilson. He had known him ever since he could remember; and though he had reason to believe him human, in common with the rest of his fellows, his was a sanctified human nature, far above the highest of what the world calls morality.

The doctor retired to rest, but could not dismiss his thoughts. What if religion were true after all! and certainly his reasons for doubting it were fast melting away. How terrible must be the condition of him who turns a deaf ear to its claim! If it were any thing, it was every thing; and no one could afford to trifle with it. How criminal seemed his own indifference during all of his life! Eternity! Who could doubt it? And where was he to spend it? But his mind was dark, his heart was cold, and it seemed impossible to get rid of his doubts.

The next morning, he rose with a faint breath of prayer in his heart, "Lord, if religion be true, make me to know it in my own experience."

Several days passed; and the anxiety increased hourly. The first feeble desire had become an agony. The whole soul was being roused from its slumbers of a life-time, and was amazed and alarmed at a sense of its condition. The doctor felt that his whole being was out of harmony, that his spiritual nature was perishing with hunger, that his whole life had been one of ingratitude and sin. Only a few days before, he would have prided himself in his morality: now what deeds he once thought virtuous seemed but refined forms of selfishness,—whited sepulchres, beautiful without, but within full of all uncleanness.

It was Saturday night; and, though three days and nights in distress had passed, he had opened his heart to no one. Now he determined to make known his feelings to Miss Elliott, and to ask her sympathy and prayers.

"I must ask a favor of you," said he to her, after

trying several hours to summon courage to mention the matter. "I need your prayers. I have spent my life as if there were no God, I have trifled with religious convictions, and trampled on the blood of the Son of God."

Miss Elliott was not altogether surprised at this frank confession of the doctor. She knew his nature, and had read his anxious thoughts in his countenance and in his actions.

"My prayers are but feeble," she replied; "but nothing in all the world could give me such pleasure as to comply with your request."

They kneeled down, and she led in prayer; after which the doctor followed, in language as simple as that of a little child, and with many tears. Seldom, indeed, is a man so wholly broken down in penitence before God.

"I have made my will," said he to Miss Elliott, as they rose from their knees.

Miss Elliott was puzzled. What could he mean?

She looked at him with a vague look of inquiry.

"Don't be perplexed," said he. "I'm in my right mind. I simply mean I have yielded up all to God,—soul, body, and property,—every thing. Henceforth, I hope to have no will but his,—to hold nothing as my own."

"Thank God!" exclaimed Miss Elliott. "The great transaction is done. Continue in simple trust, and all shall be well."

The doctor retired. He was in no ecstasy; but Christ had spoken peace to his troubled heart, and there was a great calm. He slept a sweet and dreamless sleep and waked to see the happiest morning of his life. The sun had just risen, and was pouring a flood of golden light through his chamber-window. "What has Christ done for me?" was his first thought. Ah! truly, life is a world of beauty; and that life crowned with loving-kindness and tender mercies, but, above all, spiritual life in Christ, *eternal* life through heaven's greatest sacri-

223

fice,—all this was his as a gift. So tender and delightful were his meditations that he wept for joy.

That Sabbath, the first day of Dr. Sprague's new life, was indeed a happy one; not only on account of the joyful experience it brought, but as the earnest and emblem of that Sabbath of rest which is eternal.

CHAPTER XXIII.

A House of Worship.

SUMMER and autumn had passed away, and the cold storms of winter had fully set in. The new converts had been added to the church, and greatly increased the moral forces in the community; for they carried their enterprise into their religion. The temporary log school-house had also served the purpose of a place of worship, but was very crowded, and not at all convenient: so it was decided to put up a building that would accommodate both the school and the church. An admirable plan of a building was got up by Mr. Alton and the doctor, which was to contain two apartments—the front being the chapel for church and Sunday school, and the rear a suite of rooms for the common school, which had now become so large as to require several departments. Mr. Alton had secured the interest of the iron company in the project, and the whole community was contributing liberally: so it was hoped that early the next spring they would be able to enter the new building. And this hope was daily strengthened, as timber, stone, and the various material necessary, gradually accumulated about the site chosen for the enterprise. Besides, Mr. Alton frequently announced that the whole plan was moving on without hindrance.

CHAPTER XXIV.

A Strange Accident.

LL men think all men mortal but themselves." That saying is especially true of those who are least prepared for death. There was not a child at the harbor who would not have pointed out Sandy as the wickedest man in the place, so well was he known as unscrupulous, profane, and selfish. If Death were considerate of men's preparation for the next world, or took into account their desire to depart, surely he would have been the last one summoned from that community; but he was the first victim of the King of Terrors.

227

Mr. Alton had given him permission to cut down a favorite tree belonging to the Iron Company, for the purpose of repairing his boat. At a certain time, Sandy had felled the tree; but, in falling it had left a limb hanging high in the top of a neighboring tree, and directly over the spot where he must work up the log before moving it. He spied the danger, and left his work, thinking that ere long some favoring wind would remove it. Frequently he went to the place, hoping to secure the much-desired stick of timber, but as often was warned away by the threatening limb still hanging in the air. Again and again the boat had been temporarily repaired, until a year had passed.

Now Sandy felt secure. The limb that had hung so long would still hang while he could secure the tree he so much desired. Vain hope. That limb was the appointed instrument of his death. He had scarcely struck the first blow on the felled tree which had so long waited for him, when a light breeze,—a mere breath, compared with the storms that had rocked those woods in the year that had passed—dislodged the fatal bough, and Sandy received his death-blow.

He was found senseless, but after a time came to himself; and, notwithstanding the severe fracture of his head, continued rational for several days, when the pale messenger numbered him with "the silent multitude."

He was discovered soon after the accident, and carried to his house. It was evident to all that he had but a short time to live; and there was scarcely a person at the harbor so wholly regardless of eternity as not to tremble for his future.

Sandy, however, scarcely uttered a word beside his brief account of the way in which the accident had occurred; and, when Mr. Harris called to do the part of a Christian minister in such a sad case, he refused to answer a single question, or hold any conversation whatever. In fact, scarcely any one was tolerated at his bedside but Mr. Williams.

Two days had passed, and it was evident that the sufferer could not hold out much longer. Mr. Williams had stood by him ever since he had been carried home, longing to point him to the better land, and to Him who is "The Way, the Truth, and the Life." At length the opportunity came. Sandy's quiet must not be mistaken for thoughtlessness. His whole life was before him, and he was all absorbed in reflections.

There was a sharp twinge of pain, and a deep groan; and he turned over, fixing an earnest and bewildered look on Mr. Williams, who bent over him in kindly attention.

"Hark! I has sometin' to say," said he to Mr. Williams, when he had looked around the room, and had assured himself that no one else could hear him. "My life, you know, it's wicked,—dreadful. I hasn't told no one here; but I s'pose He knows it," pointing upwards. "You know what you reads, long time ago?"

Mr. Williams was puzzled to recall what the speaker referred to.

"Dat first night at my house, you know, you read from de Holy Book," continued Sandy.

"Can you remember any thing I read?" inquired Mr. Williams.

"Darkness an' light alike to Him," repeated Sandy with emphasis as he looked upward with an expression of awe. "On de sea He is; a bed in Hell, an' on dere He is."

Mr. Williams recognized the imperfect quotations as parts of the hundred and thirty-ninth Psalm, which he had read at family prayers the first night he spent under Sandy's roof.

Sandy then told him how, at that moment, the psalm had fallen like a flood of light on his past life, setting forth all his crimes in their true colors; how that fearful revelation of himself had followed him ever since; and how he feared to cross the dark river alone, not knowing where his soul would be landed.

Then he beckoned to Mr. Williams to come still nearer, and with feeble breath, scarcely above a whisper, gave an outline of his life. That life was a shocking tale. Born and bred amidst the lowest vices of a European city, he had chosen a sea-faring life as a pirate; and Mr. Williams's blood chilled at the accounts of robbery and murder in which he had been partaker.

"Does you believe *He'll* have mercy on one dat's done de likes of sich?" inquired the dying man, with a terrified look that pierced Mr. Williams to the heart.

"When Christ was put to death on the cross," said Mr. Williams, "two robbers were crucified with him,—the one at his right hand, the other at his left. As they hung on their crosses, their living flesh nailed to the wood, the one all unconscious of the guilt of his life, as he writhed and shrieked under his tortures, railed at the Son of God in language of bitter contempt. The other, filled with bitter sorrow for his sins, and convinced of the innocency of Christ, and of his divine nature, said, 'Lord when thou comest into thy kingdom, remember me.' Jesus had compassion on him, and answered, 'To-day shalt thou be with me in Paradise.' Such is Christ's salvation. Even in that last hour, the vilest sinner was made a saint."

"May *I* hope, den?"

"Certainly, if you will but trust."

"Only trust?"

"*Only trust.* That is all God asks of the worst of men; and the best can do no more."

Mr. Williams saw that Sandy could speak but few words more. His eyes were glassy, the cold sweat of death was on his brow, and the beating of his heart began to falter. Every effort was made to point the dying man to the Lamb of God. The family was called in to receive his last words,—words of warning, feebly and brokenly uttered; and, in a few minutes the spirit had departed to "That undiscovered country from whose bourn no traveller returns."

CHAPTER XXV.

What Hope?

"WHAT hope is there?" inquired Mr. Harris, as he entered the death-chamber, just after the body had been laid out.

"It is difficult to say," replied Mr. Williams, as he made the last effort to close the sightless eyes. "He seemed to trust in the Saviour; but it was so near his last breath, that it was scarcely possible to discern the effect on his consciousness."

"Charity hopeth all things," continued Dr.

Sprague, who, in company with Mr. Williams, had dressed for the last time those wounds against whose fatal power he had striven so faithfully from the first. "Happily, we are not called on to sit in council on the future appointments of the dead. I hope with all my heart that it is well with Sandy; but the result of my observation of sick-bed repentances has not been very flattering. Through many years of medical practice, I have been accustomed to note the persons supposed to be on a death-bed, and to have repented in the eleventh hour, but that afterwards recovered; and, out of more than three-score, only three have, as far as I can judge, given evidence of a new life."

"For that reason," added Mr. Harris, "I say but little of the dead on funeral occasions. In very many cases, the hope of friends for the departure rests on some circumstance of the death-chamber rather than on living piety. To extol such a hope is to encourage men to neglect religion in life, and to trust to the uncertain emotions of a sick-bed. Moreover, to magnify the scanty virtues of the dead is unnecessary. If their life has been noble and faithful, that life has written its own history in the hearts of the people, on tablets more enduring than monuments of marble; and, if life has been a failure, no eloquence of a funeral oration can change the facts."

"I regret that I was not here when Sandy died," continued Dr. Sprague. "I think I have discovered a fact concerning death which I should like to have tested in his case. Long observation has convinced me, that there are two ways in which people die. There seems to be a point in the trying hour where the individual discovers his destiny. In some cases, it is much clearer than in others. At that point, some desire to go forward, others to come back. The former I have observed to be the Christian, the latter the sinner."

"How strange that you were not a Christian long

ago, doctor!"

"When the heart is unwilling to submit to the truth, external evidences are readily set aside," replied the doctor.

All that was possible had been done for the deceased and his family; and our friends separated, thankful that the judgment of all men is committed to an infinitely just and merciful God.

CHAPTER XXVI.

The Funeral, and What Followed.

ANDY'S funeral was an important event at the harbor. Though not influential, circumstances had rendered him a person of note. He was the oldest resident, had always occupied some public place, and was wholly unlike any other man both in personal appearance and in character. Scarcely any one else in all the community would have been so much missed alike by old and young.

There was no hearse to bear away his remains, no long procession of carriages to follow him. The coffin was placed on a bier, and borne on the shoulders of four men, while the four oldest men in the village served as pall-bearers; and nearly the whole town accompanied the widow and her family to the grave a-foot.

On the lofty elevation that overlooked the harbor from the main-land, and could be seen for many miles out upon the lake, was selected a spot of ground for a graveyard,—that second residence for every community,—and for Sandy was made out the first title.

A death in the family! who does not know its strange and awful influence? How all the affairs of life are arrested, as if by a sudden shock, until the gates of death open to receive the one who goes out from us to return no more, leaving the circle broken, the relations of the household in ghastly ruin, and hearts bleeding and torn. How sadly, almost hopelessly, do we betake ourselves to adjust the shattered remnants of home, to provide for the

240

breeches that are irreparable, and to meet the routine of daily life as a stern matter of fact!

Sandy's widow had long been the victim of care and sorrow; and, through the years of darkness and of storm, she had been trying to bear her burden alone. Now she resolved to cast it on the Lord.

It was the first evening after the funeral. The widow and her children were gathered about the fireside, and with sad faces, and tones almost hushed to a whisper, talked of the mournful event, the shadow of which hung so darkly over them.

"We must lead a better life," said the mother. "Think how wicked we has been. None, except Harry, has prayed. It's high time we all begins. Git your good book, Harry, an' rade a bit."

Harry took down his pocket-Bible, which Mr. Williams had presented him soon after his conversion, and read; after which, at his mother's request, he led in prayer. Then she followed, and afterward Tom and Frank, in short, broken sentences, and with many tears.

Harry was delighted. To hear his own mother's voice in prayer! and to hear Tom and Frank! How he had longed for it!

"I'm so happy!" he exclaimed, as he rose from his knees. "God has heard my prayer."

This was truly an era in the household. The prayers just offered were no mere form, the result of no mere temporary excitement, but of thorough consecration.

How great the change since Mr. Williams's first night under this roof! "He that goeth forth and weepeth, bearing precious seed, shall doubtless come again rejoicing, and bringing his sheaves with him."

CHAPTER XXVII.

A Noble Effort.

THE sincerity of a community in a noble cause is to be measured by its effort. Mere profession may come from impulse, or even from policy; but solid labor, for that which is benevolent comes only from conviction.

The Christians at the harbor could afford to be tried by the standard of *work*: to this, every department of spiritual enterprise could testify. But the chief object about which gathered both their thought and labor was the new house of worship. During all the winter, the work had gone on. When spring opened, every thing was on the ground, ready to proceed to erecting the building.

It was now early in May, and the building was already up, and very nearly done outside; but the community seemed about exhausted. The members and friends of the church had repeated their contributions, both in labor and in money, till it seemed impossible to collect any thing more; and yet there stood the building without windows, without plastering, and without seats; while the old temporary place of worship was so crowded, and so out of repair, as to be utterly insufficient and uncomfortable.

What was to be done? Some of the members were much disheartened, and all were perplexed. Deacon Forbes, the chairman of the building committee, was especially blue; and gave it out, as his opinion, that the work would have to be abandoned till some more favorable time in the future. "Money had never been so tight since he could remember," he said; "and the probability was, that it would yet be a good deal tighter." True it was, that times were especially hard, on account of the general falling in the market, which followed high prices during the war; and, as depression of spirits is very contagious, the deacon very soon inoculated the older part of the community.

But there were some brave souls who kept up their courage in the dark hour. Mr. Williams, especially, thought he had known times when God had delivered his people out of even greater difficulties; and Toodie, whose whole soul was in the work, declared the church was not yet as badly off as the children of Israel, with the mountains on either side of them, the Red Sea before them, and the armies of Egypt following up in the rear.

"I believe I see a way to get into the chapel for

worship next Sunday, and of making it quite comfortable in a few weeks," said Mr. Williams, on meeting Deacon Forbes one Monday morning, when the crowded and inconvenient condition of the place of worship the Sabbath before was fresh in the deacon's mind.

"Are you crazy?" inquired the deacon, eyeing Mr. Williams half in earnest and half in joke. "I guess we'd better make out your papers for the insane asylum."

"I know what I say," continued Mr. Williams, "I believe it can be done."

"How?" continued the deacon in his sceptical tone.

"I can get that large front window among the children: then a few of us can club together, and get several more. That will give sufficient light for the present, and the rest of the window-places can be filled up till some future time. The plastering we can forego for the present. We can get planks or slabs, and set them up on pins for temporary seats. The stove can be taken out of our present place of worship; and some of us can lend one or two more. I have one that is ready for service any time. I'll take the one in our parlor, and do without a parlor for the present."

"Ha, Ha, Ha!" laughed the deacon. "That sounds just like some of your wild notions, Brother Williams. How much do you suppose you can raise among the children? That front window will cost about thirty dollars. And what will you do with the window-places till windows can be procured, even admitting your plan to be a success?"

"As for raising thirty dollars among the children, I'm willing to try that; and, for the present, we can stretch cloth across the window-places."

"Very well. Go ahead, and see what can be done," added the deacon, as he turned upon his heel and walked off with a most sceptical air.

Mr. Williams's plan was no mere dream: he had

thought it out soberly and with prayer, and immediately set himself to work to put it into execution.

When Saturday afternoon came, the deacon, as well as the rest of his friends, was convinced that part, at least, of Mr. Williams's plan was not impractical. The white cotton-cloth stretched across several of the window-places admitted a genial light, and kept out the wind; while the rest were shut up. The temporary seats had been arranged according to Mr. Williams's suggestion; and, in addition to his stove and the one in the schoolhouse, several others had been brought. Of all this, and the probable comfort of the place the deacon was fully satisfied, as he locked the door about sunset, and walked down to the store to announce the change in the place of worship for the next Sabbath morning.

Never had Mr. Williams closed a week with greater satisfaction. He had found a fresh illustration of the old proverb, "Where there is a will, there is a way." And he was learning its philosophy: for he saw in the first place, that when one is in earnest in a good cause, and ready to make sacrifice, he will find abundant sympathy and help in others, even in those from whom he would not expect it; and, in the second place that "*God* helps him who helps himself," and that his resources are infinite. He thanked God, and took courage.

The sun rose clear and beautiful on Sabbath morning, and everything seemed to partake of the waking-up and the balmy freshness of spring. To the wise, Nature is full of symbols, and speaks with many voices; and spring, with its vigorous germs and budding promises is the season of hope. Mr. Williams, so full of sympathy and devotion, was highly susceptible of the subtle influences about him; and his heart welled over with joyful anticipation as Nature seemed to say, "As the rain cometh down, and the snow from heaven, and returneth not thither, but watereth the earth, and maketh it bring forth and bud, that it may give seed to the sower, and bread to the eater, so shall my word be that goeth forth out of my mouth: it shall not return unto me void, but it shall accomplish that which I please; and it shall prosper in the thing whereto I sent it. For ye shall go out with joy, and be led forth with peace: the mountains and the hills shall break forth before you into singing, and all the trees of the field shall clap their hands."

The change of place for the Sunday school had become thoroughly known; and, when the hour arrived, the new building was nearly full. It was a truly romantic occasion, and every one seemed happy over the great step forward that had been taken. Mr. Williams smiled on the teachers, and the teachers smiled on the children, and the children smiled on everybody.

Just before the close of school, Mr. Williams brought forward his plan. He rose to speak with Deacon Forbes right before him, who was watching every movement with the utmost curiosity.

"Well, children, how do you like the new house?" he inquired, with an air so cheerful and a voice so pleasant that the whole school could but answer.

"First-rate," chimed a full chorus of voices.

"Well done," added Mr. Williams. "You cannot think how happy I am to know you are pleased. Very true, the seats are rough and without backs; but we shall have better by and by: the walls, too, are homely; but they will grow smoother and brighter in time. What do you think of the windows?"

"They're pretty cool," called out Carrie Kimball, a cute little girl of about four years, who sat near enough to one of the large pieces of cotton-cloth to testify that it was not proof against the cold.

"No doubt they are somewhat cool, my little girl; but they are the best we could do for to-day.

For the future, however, I think we can do better. Do you see that large window-place in front?"

Every eye turned in the direction pointed out.

"I believe the boys and girls of our Sunday school can put in that window," continued the speaker. "It will cost thirty dollars; and, as we have a hundred scholars, it will come to just thirty cents for each. Who is there here that cannot earn thirty cents in the next six weeks? Remember, we want every child to *earn* it. If the plan can be undertaken, the factory will put in the window before next Sunday, and wait the six weeks for their pay. If the children will put in this window, the rest of us will put in some more; and so on, until they are all in. And what a noble work it will be!"

Mr. Williams had touched the hearts of the whole school. Every eye sparkled with interest. Such enthusiasm never was seen in the school before.

"How many will undertake this noble work?"

inquired Mr. Williams. "As many as will may hold up their right hands."

Immediately the chapel bristled with eager little hands. Every right hand went up.

"In order to strengthen your noble resolution, made so generously," said Mr. Williams, "each teacher may act as treasurer for his class; and, taking down the names and the amounts to be paid, will hand the money over to the regular treasurer of the Sunday school as fast as it may be brought in."

Forthwith the teachers addressed themselves to the work assigned them, and found every child ready to do his part. Some did more than was required. Miss Elliott's class was especially generous. Some of her boys put down *fifty* cents instead of thirty; and Frank Williams and the young Sandys, who were leading spirits in the noble little company, put down *a dollar a piece.*

Mr. Williams was cheered with the success of his plan; and the children never had felt so happy in their lives before.

Every good and noble effort has its influence. When the children had got through their pledges, Deacon Forbes, whose doubts and misgivings had all vanished, rose, and proposed that the teachers and friends of the school pledge themselves for another window, to be paid for in six weeks. Immediately the papers were circulated; and, when the subscriptions were counted up, instead of one window, the pledges were sufficient for three.

Then Mr. Williams proposed to sing the doxology; and, when the school dispersed, it was difficult to tell who carried home the happiest hearts, the old people or the children.

CHAPTER XXVIII.

A Grand Success.

CHILDREN are an element of power in a community. Their young natures are not only susceptible of impulse and enthusiasm, but of determination and perseverance. On Monday morning, the people at the harbor felt that a new spirit of enterprise was abroad among them. All the boys and girls of the place were looking for work; and their ambition was almost unbounded. Boys of ten and twelve years, who had never been thought sufficient for a day's work of any kind, felt competent for almost any ordinary employment. Little girls, who had never so much as washed the dishes or swept the kitchen, hired themselves out for small jobs of washing, bits of sewing, and nursing babies. It was not long before every boy and girl in the Sunday school had found something to do, and was laying up something for the window. Before the first week had passed, Mr. Williams was greeted with many favorable reports. Some of the boys were driving cows to pasture, for which they were receiving a cent a day; others carried warm dinners to men working in the woods, for which they were paid regularly; others drove teams and made gardens; while some had special success, and earned ten or twenty-five cents in a single job. And the girls were quite as successful as the boys. They hemmed nearly all the handkerchiefs in town, sewed rags for carpets, pieced quilts, and filled little vacancies without number, both in kitchen and parlor. The community was astonished at the amount of work the children could do.

Mr. Williams saw that it was safe to order the window; and, at the time appointed, it was paid for. Of course, the teachers and friends were equally prompt in fulfilling their pledges; and, at the end of the six weeks referred to, all the windows were in the chapel: for Miss Elliott had canvassed the community outside of the church and Sunday school, and had found everybody, even the worst men in town, ready to do something for the work.

Mr. Henry said he didn't see how any could refuse to give towards a cause that was doing so much good, especially when the children were doing so nobly for it.

CHAPTER XXIX.

Conclusion.

year had passed,—a happy year to the church and Sunday school at the harbor; for it was one of labor and success. The church had grown to a membership of forty; and they were harmonious, spiritual-minded, and enterprising. The Sunday school numbered a hundred and thirty regular attendants, and was constantly increasing in interest and power; for the superintendent was earnest and wide awake, keeping himself posted in Sabbath-school improvements, and adopting the best principles: the teachers were prompt, studious, and prayerful; and the children appreciated their advantages, and brought every one they could find into the school. The chapel was finished, including the schoolrooms; and the school, devotional meetings of the week, and Sabbath school and preaching on the Lord's Day, kept it in constant service.

In short, a great work had been done in the community. Every kind of vice had been put to shame; and the tone of morality and public sentiment, once so low, was now fully equal to that of the first order of Christian communities. As far as possible, all labor was suspended, on the Sabbath: pleasure-excursions were entirely abandoned, and there was a general and punctual attendance at the house of God. As a general thing, the Christians of the place did not complain of coldness of heart in the Lord's work; for they had learned a universal remedy for that disorder, namely, *labor and sacrifice*. This was their motto; and Miss Elliott, with her usual skill and taste, had represented it beautifully on a large shield: on it was the picture of an altar, with a lamb for its sacrifice, and a ploughman at work in his field; while at the bottom of it, in large gold letters, were the words, *"Ready for either."* This was placed in the chapel, high on the wall back of the desk, and rested on our country's coat of arms and on the beautiful folds of the "stars and stripes."

This motto was well carried out. Each teacher in the Sunday school was the captain of a company, the superintendent and the church-officers were colonels and majors, and the pastor was commander-in-chief.

"Freely ye have received, freely give." This principle was fully applied by the people at the harbor. They did not believe in talking and praying, while they withheld tithes and offerings. Mr. Williams was the treasurer of the church and congregation; and he considered the financial education of a Christian community a matter of the most vital importance. The expenses necessary for the year were accurately calculated, and placed before every individual as a matter of *debt,* not of *charity.* "A man should pay his honest debts without complaint," he said. And if any still persisted in calling the payment of his debt a gift, he taught him to give cheerfully, to know the blessedness of giving. "For giving," said he, "is heaven's law, and the law of nature. He who does not give is a monster, a contradiction to the world in which he lives." Mr. Williams's doctrine was true, and carried conviction.

"I'm not a Christian, an' more's the pity for it," said Mr. Henry one day to Dr. Sprague; "but I al'ays feel better after handin' over to Williams my part for the good cause. An' I'm not the only one that feels so. I was down in the store t'other evenin', when he came in with his subscription-paper; an' nearly every one forked over to him, an' seemed to feel the better for it. An' there's old Toodie; why, I jes seed her shed tears t'other day for clear joy, when she handed him her 'mite,' as she called it; an' a pretty good mite it was, too, I tell ye, for a poor woman. Well then, there's the children. Every boy in the Sunday school earns somethin' to pay for the preachin', an' goes to church every time with all the interest of a stock-holder. An' jes the same with the girls. If a feller has any soul, givin' makes him feel good, no mis-take; an' I don't know but it 'ud help grow a soul, if he hadn't none."

We have traced the history of the harbor from a single family to a thrifty business community of five hundred inhabitants, and now it becomes a county-seat. We have seen it in its intellectual and moral darkness and degradation; and we have seen the introduction of the gospel, and watched the development of its elevating and purifying princi-ples, until the church has become a regenerating power, not only in its own community, but for many miles beyond. For Mr. Alton and Dr. Sprague, with the aid of others interested in the

Lord's work, are establishing mission interests in several of the adjoining settlements. Sunday schools and prayer meetings are henceforth to be held there; and Mr. Harris will have regular appointments for preaching.

Truly the beautiful prophecy of old has been fulfilled in its highest moral and spiritual sense,— "Then the eyes of the blind shall be opened, and the ears of the deaf shall be unstopped. Then shall the lame man leap as an hart, and the tongue of the dumb sing: for in the wilderness shall waters break out, and streams in the desert. And the parched ground shall become a pool, and the thirsty land springs of water."

Truly the gospel is Heaven's greatest gift to man; and how ungrateful is he who turns a deaf ear to its call!

THE END

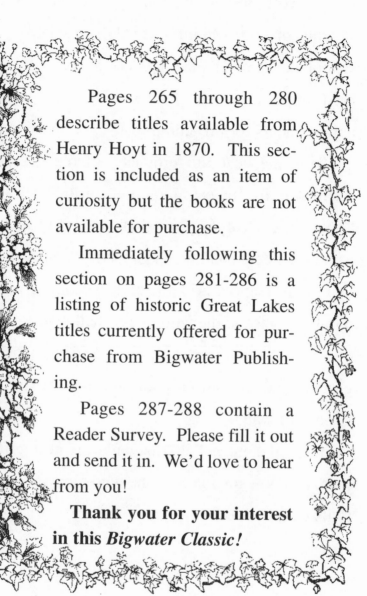

Pages 265 through 280 describe titles available from Henry Hoyt in 1870. This section is included as an item of curiosity but the books are not available for purchase.

Immediately following this section on pages 281-286 is a listing of historic Great Lakes titles currently offered for purchase from Bigwater Publishing.

Pages 287-288 contain a Reader Survey. Please fill it out and send it in. We'd love to hear from you!

Thank you for your interest in this *Bigwater Classic!*

ɪLLUSTRATED ᵂORKS

PUBLISHED BY

HENRY HOYT,

9 CORNHILL, BOSTON.

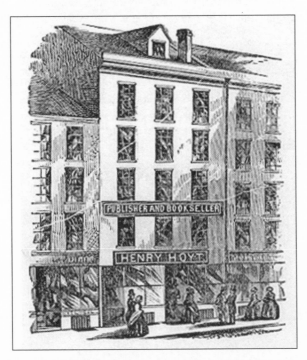

The publications of Mr. HOYT are gotten up in substantial elegance, and are beautifully illustrated. Free from all sectarianism, they are yet eminently evangelical in character and spirit; and no safer or better works for the Sunday school or family are known to the Christian public than the issues of this house.

BOTH SIDES OF THE STREET.

Price $1.60

Out of over three hundred manuscripts presented in competition, the writer of this most interesting and instructive work was awarded the first prize of six hundred dollars.

MOTH AND RUST.

Price $1.60

The second award, of three hundred dollars, was made to the author of this volume ; and it is a work replete with every excellence.

The clear and elevated character of these " Prize Volumes," the high moral and religious tone that pervades every page, and the unique style in which they are bound, places them far above the ordinary juvenile issues of the day.

THE ORIENT BOYS.

Price $1.50

KEPT FROM IDOLS.

A fascinating volume.
Price $1.50

THE WHOLE ARMOR.

A capital book for the family.
Price $1.25

TOM BENTLEY ; or, The Prodigal's Return.

Price $1.50

INTO THE HIGHWAYS.

Every young pastor and earnest Christian should have this latest issue from the gifted pen of Mrs. C. E. K. DAVIS.

Price $1.50

266

BOTH SIDES OF THE STREET.

By Mrs. MARY SPRING WALKER.

The first prize volume. $600 awarded.

A volume full of originality, interest, and power; yet pervaded by a deep religious sentiment.

Price $1.60

267

SNAIL-SHELL HARBOR.

Price $1.25

The scene is laid in the Lake-Superior Copper region. Well written, full of interest, while the religious element is prominent.

ELEANOR WILLOUGHBY'S SELF.

Price $1.25

Direct in its appeals, devout in its character, it cannot fail to be a help to the young Christian.

CAPTAIN JOHN.

By Mrs. ANN E. PORTER.

Price $1.50

A story of rare self-sacrifice. No one can lay down the book until the last word is read.

QUEEN RHODA.

Price $1.50

The weakness of our own strength is clearly shown forth in this charming work, whether in the inward growth in grace, or in our power amid outward trials.

AUNT REBEKAH'S CHARGE.

Price $1.50

No goodness can be otherwise than spasmodic and transient which is not based on a prayerful desire to serve God.

CHARITY HURLBURT. A Book for Young Misses.

Price $1.50

School-life faithfully portrayed. The religious power by which even the very young may come out of its trials victorious, truthfully described.

THE OLD OAK FARM.

From the London Sunday School Union.

Price $1.00

A LOST PIECE OF SILVER; or, Struggles into a Better Life.

MOTH AND RUST; or, A Very Plain Tale.

The second prize volume. $300 awarded.

A book greatly needed, and should be in every family and Sunday
school in the land.

Price $1.60

WHICH WINS.
Especially for Boys.
Price $1.50

NANNY DAVENPORT.
A charming book for Misses.
Price $1.50

JESSIE GORDON.
Price $1.50

THE MOUNTAIN PATRIOTS. A Tale of Savoy.
Price $1.50

DONAT CLAIR, THE MANUSCRIPT MAN.
Price $1.25

MILDRED GWYNNE.
Price $1.25

LINSIDE FARM.
Price $1.25

THE UPWARD PATH. A Temperance Tale.
Price $1.25

CAPT. RUSSELL'S WATCHWORD.
Price $1.25

THE VEIL LIFTED; or, Romance and Reality of Convent Life.
Price $1.15

THE WHOLE ARMOR.

THEREBY SAVED FROM TEMPTATION.

A very interesting story, with a grand temperance lesson. Natural in its description, and full of wholesome truths.

Price $1.25

THE OLD RED HOUSE.
A splendid work for the family.
Price $1.50

THE SQUIRE'S DAUGHTER.
For Young Ladies.
Price $1.25

EUGENE COOPER.
Price $1.15

MARK STEADMAN ; or, Show Your Colors.
Price $1.15

THE CHILD MARTYR, AND EARLY CHRIS-TIAN HEROES OF ROME.
Price $1.15

BERTIE'S BIRTHDAY PRESENT.
Price $1.15

THE CORNER STALL.
Price $1.15

TIM, THE SCISSORS GRINDER.
By MADELINE LESLIE.
Price $1.25

OTHER BOOKS BY THE SAME AUTHOR.

Sequel to Tim $1.25	The Prize Bible $1.15
Tim's Sister 1.25	Little Rag Pickers 60
White and Black Lies . . 1.25	The Bound Boy 55
Every-Day Duties . . . 1.25	The Bound Girl 55
Light and Shade 1.25	Virginia 55
The Organ Grinder . . . 1.15	The Prairie Flower 55

272

UNDER THE CROSS.

One of the beautiful books of the season, every way tasteful and elegant. Its subjects relate almost wholly to that sublimest theme, THE CROSS OF OUR LORD JESUS CHRIST.

As a presentation volume, or an aid to private devotion, these sacred lyrics will be found most fittingly adapted.

Holiday Edition, on heavy toned paper, English cloth,
full gilt, nineteen illustrations $4.25
The same in Turkey morocco extra . . . . . 5.50 to 8.00
 "   "   " (Levant) 9.00
Small Edition, cloth, four illustrations 1.50
 "   " Turkey morocco 4.50

BABY'S CHRISTMAS.

Plate paper, thirty-three illustrations, gilt, $1.25.
 "   "   "   " plain, 1.00.

THE COURT AND CAMP OF DAVID,

Royal Octavo Edition, sixteen illustrations. $2.50.
Sunday-school Edition, four illustrations. $1.50.

273

HE THAT OVERCOMETH ; or, A Conquering Gospel.

By the author of " The Higher Christian Life."

Price $1.75

THE HIGHER CHRISTIAN LIFE.

By Rev. W. E. BOARDMAN.

Price $1.50

MILLENNIAL EXPERIENCE ; or, God's Will Known and Done.

By Rev. A. UNDERWOOD.

Price $1.50

NATURAL THEOLOGY.

By Dr. MAHAN.

Price $2.00

THE HARVEST-WORK OF THE HOLY SPIRIT.

By Rev. E. P. HAMMOND.

Price $1.25

OTHER WORKS BY THE SAME AUTHOR.

Little Ones in the Fold $0.90
The Better Life, and How to Find it 80
Child's Guide to Heaven 35
The Revival Melodist 15

The Blood of Jesus. . . $0.40   Look to Jesus. $0.40
Hope in Jesus 40   The Gift of Jesus 40

JESSICA'S FIRST PRAYER.

From the London Religious Tract Society.   Price 75 cents.

BY THE SAME AUTHOR.

The Prize Library.

(1867.)

Five Volumes. $7.00.

Culm Rock.

Tip Lewis and his Lamp.

Carl's Home.

After Years.

Old Sunapee.

The Golden Library.

Four Volumes. $6.00.

By Mrs. J. McNair Wright.

The Golden Work.

The Golden Life.

The Golden Heart.

The Golden Fruit.

The Temperance Library.

Four Volumes. $5.75.

John and the Demijohn.

The Family Doctor.

The Old Distillery.

The Upward Path.

The Teetotaller's Library.

Five Volumes. $2.50.

Taking a Stand.

First Glass of Wine.

Hemlock Ridge.

John Lennard.

Violet.

TOM BENTLEY.

The whole story is pervaded by a fervent Christian spirit, and is the narrative of an actual experience.

Price $1.50

The Social Library.

Six Volumes. $6.00.

The Banished Daughter.
Stories from Life.
Parable of the Rain-Drop.

New Stories.
Philip Martin.
Caleb White.

A mine of anecdote.

The Maidie Library.

Six Volumes. $5.25.

Little Maidie. Part I.
" " Part II.
" " Part III.

Jenny's Geranium.
A Christmas Story.
Daisy Bright.

The Jessica Library.

Six Volumes. $4.25.

Jessica's First Prayer.
Jessica's Mother.
Kate and her Brother.

Emily's Bracelet.
Music Governess.
Ellen Vincent.

The Tim Series.

Three Volumes. $3.75.

Tim the Scissors-Grinder.
Tim's Sister.

Sequel to Tim.

The Child's Bible Stories.

Four Volumes. $3.25.

A charming set, written expressly for small children, by Mrs. C. K. Davis.

278

THE ORIENT BOYS.

Every page full of interest and instruction. The most capital boy-book of the season.

Price $1.50

The Fifty-Volume Library.

A SPLENDID SELECTION OF CHOICE READING.

Fifty Volumes, 18mo, cloth, $20.00.

The Mountain Gems.

Four Volumes. $2.50.

By Rev. JOHN TODD, D.D.

Cush Going to Mill.	Uncle Ben and Uncle Levi.
Shaking Out the Reef.	The Mother Dove.

The Sunbeam Library.

Six Volumes, $2.50.

Mabel's Pets.	Norah's Lilies.
The Morning Hour.	Nellie Wells.
The Dead Monkey.	Molly's Verse.

Nearly one hundred illustrations.

The Choice Little Library.

Six Volumes. $2.50.

Emma Herbert.	Ned Graham.
Ivan.	The Fairest Rose.
Eddie and May.	Little Kit.

Nearly one hundred illustrations.

Choice Reading for the Little Ones.

My Pet Library.	640 pages.	10 volumes.	$2.25.
The Little Home Library.	640 pages.	10 volumes.	$2.25.
The Little Folks' Library.	640 pages.	10 volumes.	$2.25.
The Welcome Library.	640 pages.	10 volumes.	$2.25.
The Little Ones' Library.	640 pages.	10 volumes.	$2.25.

Great Lakes Romances®

Wholesome Fiction for Women

For pricing and availability of the following titles, contact:

Bigwater Publishing
P.O. Box 177
Caledonia, MI 49316

Mackinac, First in the series of *Great Lakes Romances*® (Set at Grand Hotel, Mackinac Island, 1895.) Victoria Whitmore is no shy, retiring miss. When her father runs into money trouble, she heads to Mackinac Island to collect payment due from Grand Hotel for the furniture he's made. But dealing with Rand Bartlett, the hotel's manager, poses an unexpected challenge. Can Victoria succeed in finances without losing her heart?

The Captain and the Widow, Second in the series of *Great Lakes Romances®* (Set in South Haven, Michigan, 1897.) Lily Atwood Haynes is beautiful, intelligent, and alone at the helm of a shipping company at the tender age of twenty. Then Captain Hoyt Curtiss offers to help her navigate the choppy waters of widowhood. Together, can they keep a new shipping line—and romance—afloat?

Sweethearts of Sleeping Bear Bay, Third in the series of *Great Lakes Romances®* (Set in the Sleeping Bear Dune region of northern Michigan, 1898.) Mary Ellen Jenkins has successfully mastered the ever-changing shoals and swift currents of the Mississippi, but Lake Michigan poses a new set of challenges. Can she round the ever-dangerous Sleeping Bear Point in safety, or will the steamer—and her heart—run aground under the influence of Thad Grant?

Charlotte of South Manitou Island, Fourth in the series of *Great Lakes Romances ®* (Set on South Manitou Island, Michigan, 1891-1898) Charlotte Richards, fatherless at age eleven, thought she'd never smile again. But Seth Trevelyn, son of South Manitou Island's lightkeeper, makes it his mission to show her that life goes on, and so does true friendship. Together, they explore the World's Columbian Exposition in far-away Chicago where he saves her from a near-fatal fire. When he leaves the island to create a life of his own in Detroit, he realizes Charlotte is his one true love. Will his feelings be returned when she grows to womanhood?

Aurora of North Manitou Island, Fifth in the series of *Great Lakes Romances®* (Set on North Manitou Island, Michigan, 1898-1899.) With her new husband, Harrison, lying helpless after an accident on stormy Lake Michigan, Aurora finds marriage far from the glorious romantic adventure she had anticipated. And when Serilda Anders appears out of his past to tend the light and nurse him to health, Aurora is certain her marriage is doomed. Maybe Cad Blackburn, with the ready wit and silver tongue, is the answer. But it isn't right to accept the safe harbor *he's* offering. Where is the light that will guide her through troubled waters?

Bridget of Cat's Head Point, Sixth in the series of *Great Lakes Romances®* (Set in Traverse City and the Leelanau Peninsula of Michigan, 1899-1900.) When Bridget Richards leaves South Manitou Island to take up residence on Michigan's mainland, she suffers no lack of ardent suitors. Nat Trevelyn wants desperately to make her his bride and the mother of his two-year-old son. Attorney Kenton McCune showers her with gifts and rapt attention. And Erik Olson shows her the incomparable beauty and romance of a Leelanau summer. Who will finally win her heart?

Rosalie of Grand Traverse Bay, Seventh in the series of *Great Lakes Romances®* (Set in Traverse City, Michigan, and Winston-Salem, North Carolina, 1900.) Soon after Rosalie Foxe arrives in Traverse City for the summer of 1900, she stands at the center of controversy. Her aunt and uncle are about to lose their confectionery shop, and Rosalie is being blamed. Can Kenton McCune, a handsome, Harvard-trained lawyer, prove her innocence and win her heart?

Isabelle's Inning, Encore Edition #1 in the series of *Great Lakes Romances®* (Set in the heart of Great Lakes Country,

1903.) Born and raised in the heart of the Great Lakes, Isabelle Dorlon pays little attention to the baseball players patronizing her mother's rooming house—until Jack Weatherby moves in. He's determined to earn a position with the Erskine College Purple Stockings, and a place in her heart as well, but will his affections fade once he learns the truth about her humiliating flaw?

Jenny of L'Anse Bay, Special Edition in the series of *Great Lakes Romances®* (Set in the Keweenaw Peninsula of Upper Michigan in 1867.) Eager to escape the fiery disaster that leaves her home in ashes, Jennifer Crawford sets out on an adventure to an Ojibway Mission on L'Anse Bay. In the wilderness, her affections grow for a native people very different from herself—especially for the chief's son, Hawk. Together, can they overcome the differences of their diverse cultures, and the harsh, deadly weather of the North Country?

Elizabeth of Saginaw Bay, Pioneer Edition in the series of *Great Lakes Romances®* (Set in the Saginaw Valley of Michigan, 1837.) The taste of wedding cake is still sweet in Elizabeth Morgan's mouth when she sets out with her bridegroom, Jacob, from York State for the new State of Michigan. But she isn't prepared for the untamed forest, crude lodgings, and dangerous diseases that await her there. Desperately, she seeks her way out of the forest that holds her captive, but God seems to have another plan for her future.

Sweet Clover—A Romance of the White City, Centennial Edition in the series of *Great Lakes Romances®* (Set in Chicago at the World's Columbian Exposition of 1893.)

The Fair brought unmatched excitement and wonder to Chicago, inspiring this innocent romance by Clara Louise Burnham first published in 1894. In it, Clover strives to rebuild a lifelong friendship with Jack Van Tassel, a childhood playmate who's spent several years away from the home of his youth. But The Fair lures him back, and their long-lost friendship rekindles. Can true love conquer the years that have come between, or will betrayals of the past pose impenetrable barriers?

Unlikely Duet—Caledonia Chronicles—Part 1 in the series of *Great Lakes Romances®* (Set in Caledonia, Michigan, 1905.) Caroline Chappell practiced long and hard for her recital on the piano and organ in Caledonia's Methodist Episcopal Church. She even took up the trumpet and composed a duet to perform with Joshua Bolden, an ace trumpet player whom she'd long admired. Now, two days before the performance, it looks as if her recital plans, and her relationship with Joshua are hitting sour notes. Will she be able to restore harmony in time to save her musical reputation?

Butterfly Come Home—Caledonia Chronicles—Part 2 in the series of *Great Lakes Romances®* (Set in Caledonia and Calumet, Michigan, 1905-06.) Deborah Dapprich's flighty ways had earned her the nickname, "Butterfly," in childhood. Now, as a young woman of eighteen in the year 1905, her impetuous wanderings brought unanticipated trouble. A marriage of convenience to her childhood friend seemed the only way out. Tommy Rockwell knew that life with his Butterfly would never be dull, but he wasn't prepared for the challenges of his new bride. From Caledonia to Calumet he pursued her, only to discover that he was running second to her first love, the theater. Would she ever light long enough for his love, and the will of God, to work their way into her heart?

Amelia by Brand Whitlock, Encore Edition #2 in the series of *Great Lakes Romances®* (Set in Chicago and Springfield, Illinois, 1903.) Amelia Ansley's anticipation of marriage to Morley Vernon was spoiled by only one small matter—his involvement in politics. The office of State Senator seemed unimportant and bothersome. Why couldn't he get elected to the Senate in Washington? Morley Vernon's loyalty to party politics was equaled only by his loyalty to Amelia Ansley—until Maria Burley Greene stepped into his life. This woman attorney who was also a suffragette was the embodiment of exquisite daintiness, wholly feminine and alluring. Impulsively he offered to promote her cause, only later realizing that this decision could either make or break both his political career and his relationship with Amelia.

Bigwater Classics™ **Series**
***Great Lakes Christmas Classics*, A Collection of Short Stories, Poems, Illustrations, and Humor from Olden Days**—From the pages of the *Detroit Free Press* of 1903, the Traverse City *Morning Record* of 1900, and other turn-of-the-century sources come heart-warming, rib-tickling, eye-catching gems of Great Lakes Christmases past. So sit back, put your feet up, and prepare for a thoroughly entertaining escape to holidays of old!

READER SURVEY—*Snail-Shell Harbor*

Your opinion counts! Please fill out and mail this form to:
Reader Survey
Bigwater Publishing
P.O. Box 177
Caledonia, MI 49316

Your
Name:_____

Street:_____

City,State,Zip:_____

In return for your completed survey, we will send you a bookmark and the latest issue of our newsletter. If your name is not currently on our mailing list, we will also include four note papers and envelopes of an historic Great Lakes scene (while supplies last).

1. Please check the response and share comments that best describe your reading preferences.

_____I enjoyed this book and would like to read more reprinted
        classics set in the Great Lakes.

_____I would not buy/read another similar book.

Comments:_____

_____

_____

(Survey questions continue on next page.)

3. Where did you purchase this book? (If you borrowed it from the library, please give the name/location of the library.)

_____

4. What influenced your decision to read this book?

_____Setting   _____Title

_____Other (Please describe)_____

_____

5. Please indicate your age range:

_____Under 18   _____25-34   _____46-55

_____18-24   _____35-45   _____Over 55

If desired, include additional comments below.